D0251101

THE GREAT HIBERNATION

ALSO BY TARA DAIRMAN

All Four Stars
The Stars of Summer
Stars So Sweet

the GREAT HIBERNATION

TARA DAIRMAN

ILLUSTRATIONS BY REBECCA GREEN

 Published in the United States by Wendy Lamb Books, an imprint of Random House Children's Books, a division of Penguin Random House LLC, New York.

Wendy Lamb Books and the colophon are trademarks of Penguin Random House LLC.

Visit us on the Web! randomhousekids.com

Educators and librarians, for a variety of teaching tools, visit us at RHTeachersLibrarians.com

Library of Congress Cataloging-in-Publication Data
Names: Dairman, Tara, author.
Title: The great hibernation / Tara Dairman.
Description: New York : Wendy Lamb Books, [2017] | Summary: In the tiny northern town of St. Polonius, everyone over the age of twelve falls asleep after the traditional tasting of the Sacred Bear Liver at the Founders' Day Festival, leaving the children in charge, including Jean who tries to solve the mystery.
Identifiers: LCCN 2016034600 (print) | LCCN 2017009529 (ebook) | ISBN 978-1-5247-1785-8 (trade) | ISBN 978-1-5247-1786-5 (lib. bdg.) | ISBN 978-1-5247-1788-9 (pbk.) | ISBN 978-1-5247-1787-2 (ebook)
Subjects: | CYAC: City and town life—Fiction. | Poisons—Fiction. | Mystery and detective stories.
Classification: LCC PZ7.D1521127 Gr 2017 (print) | LCC PZ7.D1521127 (ebook) | DDC [Fic]—dc23

The text of this book is set in 12-point Bembo Monotype.
Interior design by Trish Parcell

Printed in the United States of America
10 9 8 7 6 5 4 3 2 1
First Edition

FOR MY SISTER BEAR, BROOKE

COME ONE, COME ALL,

TO THE 343RD ANNUAL CELEBRATION OF

FOUNDERS' DAY!

SATURDAY, OCTOBER 14, ON THE TOWN SQUARE,
ST. POLONIUS-ON-THE-FJORD

FEATURING

THE MAJESTIC MELODIES OF THE ST. POLONIUS BRASS BAND!

A RIVETING REENACTMENT OF THE FOUNDING OF OUR TOWN
BY ST. POLONIUS PRIMARY SCHOOL'S THIRD GRADE CLASS!

A SCINTILLATING SPEECH BY MAYOR THEOBALD KING!

AND OF COURSE

THE ANNUAL TASTING OF THE SACRED BEAR LIVER!
(ALL THOSE OF AGE *MUST* PARTICIPATE)

HELP KEEP OUR TOWN'S BEAUTIFUL TRADITIONS ALIVE!

THIS YEAR'S FESTIVITIES GENEROUSLY COSPONSORED
BY THE NATIONAL THISTLEBERRY COUNCIL

CHAPTER 1

The bear was dead.

Or was supposed to be by now, anyway. The eight-year-old boy in the bear suit still danced across the stage, roaring and clutching his stomach. "ARRRR!"

In the audience, Jean Huddy stifled a laugh. She looked up at her brother, Micah, onstage in his seventeenth-century-seafarer costume. He was trying not to laugh, too.

Micah was playing Captain Polonius—the hero of *The*

Founders' Story—but everyone knew that the best role was the bear. When Jean was in third grade, it had gone to her best friend, Katrin Ash. Katrin had transformed herself into a wild animal, but now Micah's own best friend, Axel Gorson, was giving her performance a run for its money.

"AIEEEE!" With one final spin, Axel collapsed at Micah's feet. The audience cheered. Micah knelt, pulled a sponge soaked in red thistleberry juice out of a hidden pocket in the bear suit, and held the fake "liver" high up over his head. He then tore it into pieces and passed it out among his classmates, who were playing shipwrecked sailors. They pretended to gobble the liver down, chorusing "Yum!" and smiling.

The audience cheered louder, but Jean didn't join in. She knew what was coming after the play. On Founders' Day, the citizens of St. Polonius-on-the-Fjord really *did* eat a bite of bear liver—but no one said "Yum!" Bear liver smelled like a wet dog and, from what Jean had heard, tasted even worse. Every resident who was at least twelve years, four months, and six days old (as this had been the age of the youngest sailor on Captain Polonius's original crew) was required to take part in the ritual . . . and today, Jean was twelve years, four months, and nineteen days old.

It's an honor to participate—her parents had been saying this all week. Unfortunately, Jean wasn't too good at bringing honor to her family. At the school-wide spelling bee, she'd been the first student eliminated; even Micah, four years younger than she was, had lasted a few rounds. And back when she was Micah's age in *The Founders' Story,* she'd bungled her only line in front of the entire town.

This year that line belonged to Cora Buggins, a tiny seven-year-old who carried a purple stuffed narwhal everywhere she went. She had even snuck it up onstage under her sailor's coat—Jean could see its horn poking out of Cora's sleeve.

"Great saints, but I am sleepy!" the girl cried. Her voice squeaked, but at least the words made sense. Jean cringed at the memory of her own version ("Great slaints, but I am seepy!"), and the laughter that had followed.

All the little sailors onstage slumped forward and pretended to fall asleep.

The Founders' Story was an odd tale. Jean had no trouble believing that, in 1674, Captain Polonius and his crew had shipwrecked on this barren northern peninsula and started to starve as winter set in. And it made sense that Polonius would pray to the saints to use their ancient powers to save his crew. But why, of all things, would the saints send a *bear* staggering down from the mountains as a source of food? Couldn't they have simply washed fish up on the shore, or made the thistleberry bushes fruit early?

And then why, after Polonius had slain the bear, did his crew eat only its liver?

And, most importantly, how did the crew then manage to sleep through the *entire* winter without eating, drinking, or even taking shelter from the elements? Now the third graders were rubbing their eyes, pretending to wake up months later in the spring.

Jean knew the official answer.

"It's a miracle!" cried the little sailors. They declared

Captain Polonius a saint for bringing about their miraculous hibernation, and named their settlement for him. Then Micah, standing tall at center stage, declared: "Every year hence, you townsfolk will honor the founding of St. Polonius-on-the-Fjord by slaying a bear and feasting on its liver! If you don't, you'll bring the wrath of the saints on yourselves."

Next to her, Jean's mom rolled her eyes.

That morning, over toast and sheep's-milk yogurt, Mom had given Micah an earful. "Dad and I are so proud of you for winning the lead role. But don't take the story too seriously! If you ask me, it's a canoe full of codwash. Saintly magic and miracles—more like superstition and nonsense."

"Now, now," their dad had said, his thick eyebrows wagging as he reached for the smoked herring. "I wouldn't be so quick to dismiss the story. In my research, I've learned that even the tallest tales can hold a grain of truth."

Dad taught history at the town's small university extension, specializing in the sagas of the North Country. But he also loved to joke around. Jean couldn't tell if he was serious or not.

Micah looked as confused as Jean felt. "Mom . . . if you don't believe in the old stories, then why do you always eat the liver?"

Mom sighed. "It's complicated, kiddo. Traditions . . . they're still important. When your people have been doing something for generations, you don't throw that all away at once."

Jean thought about that as Micah and his class took their bows. Her parents ate the liver every year, and the fact that she was about to join them *did* mean something.

Dad reached over and squeezed Jean's hand. "You ready?" Jean nodded as volunteers began to swarm the aisles, carrying big silver bowls.

The musty odor of the liver hit her nose. She knew the smell well from past Founders' Days, and her guts twisted. For a desperate moment, she considered pulling the sleeve of her coat over the red bracelet she'd been given upon entering the tent, the one that meant she was of age. But she was sitting between her parents. Even if no one else saw her dodge the liver-tasting, they would.

Holding her breath as a silver bowl paused in front of her, she took a wooden spoon with its shiny scoop of meat.

It's just a sliver, she told herself. *A sliver of liver.* A giggle escaped her lips, and the old woman in front of her turned and frowned.

Mayor King climbed up onstage, his sallow face framed by a magnificent bear-fur collar. The audience fell silent. Jean could hear the arctic wind howling outside, but the tent was hot from the press of bodies in winter coats.

At the mayor's signal, everyone rose from their seats. "In the name of the Sailors," he intoned, "the Saints, and the Miraculous Bear!"

"In the name of the Sailors, the Saints, and the Miraculous Bear!" the crowd repeated, and then, as one, they raised their spoons to their lips. *An honor to participate,* Jean reminded herself, *and maybe curses from the saints if I don't.*

She shoved her liver as far back into her mouth as she could. If she didn't chew it, maybe she wouldn't taste it! She swallowed the bite down whole . . . and started to gag. The stuff shot back up: bitter, sour, even sickly sweet.

Stomach heaving, Jean tore out of the tent. Frigid air whipped her dark hair off her face as the liver-sliver splatted out onto a snowdrift. Her knees buckled, and she had to grab one of the tent poles to keep herself upright.

A shadow fell across the snow at her feet. Jean turned to find two familiar sets of eyes upon her.

She dropped her gaze, unable to withstand her parents' looks of surprise. St. Polonians were the descendants of great seafarers. If they weren't born with iron stomachs, they were at least supposed to have developed them by age twelve.

Jean shuffled sideways, but it was too late to hide her mess. She had faced her first test as a full-grown citizen of St. Polonius-on-the-Fjord—and she had failed.

"Are you all right?" Dad asked.

Jean nodded but couldn't meet his eyes. Every snowflake that fell on her head made her tremble harder. The Tasting of the Sacred Bear Liver was in the town charter. Any citizen who didn't complete it had to be reported to the authorities. No one had failed to eat their portion in years, but everyone knew the traditional punishment: being marooned on a slab of ice in the North Sea. Jean didn't know for how long, but it had to be long enough to appease the saints; it was long enough for one citizen in the 1800s to have lost four toes and an earlobe.

She sucked in a breath, the frosty air stinging her raw throat. "I'll turn myself in. I'll go see Mayor King."

Mom stepped forward. She was hatless, her short black hairs freezing into tiny, spiky icicles. "You'll do no such thing." She stomped her heavy work boot into the snowdrift and kicked a pile of loose snow into the hole she had created.

Just like that, all evidence of Jean's sickness was erased. "You'll do nothing," Mom continued in a hushed tone, "because *nothing happened*. Right, Brian?"

"Right," Dad said.

Jean was flabbergasted. "But the charter—"

"Curse that infernal charter!" Mom was angry-whispering now. "This town is far too obsessed with saintly nonsense. If you could see some of the other ridiculous laws that are still on the books . . ."

Dad put a calming hand on Mom's shoulder. She often got worked up about politics.

"I think Jean had the right idea today," Dad said in a lighter tone. "This year's liver tasted especially disgusting. I strongly considered throwing it up myself!"

In spite of everything, a tiny smile crossed Jean's lips.

"Still . . ." He eyed the tent flap. "I don't think anyone else in town needs to know about this."

"No," Mom said. "They don't. Jean, you'll say nothing to anyone. You promise?"

A burst of applause sounded from the tent, and Jean nodded quickly as people began to emerge. The very first person out was Magnus King, son of the mayor. Though he was Jean's classmate, they rarely spoke—which was why she was surprised when he hurried over.

"Jean!" he cried. "Are you unwell? I saw you run out of the tasting."

"Busybody," Jean's mom muttered as Magnus skidded to a stop in the snow in front of them. He was panting, and his gold spelling-bee medal bobbed up and down on his chest. He never went anywhere without that medal. Katrin called him "Magnus the Magnificent," and she didn't mean it as a compliment.

"Jean is fine," Mom said before Jean could open her mouth. "She just got a little overheated in there, right, honey?"

"Right," Jean said. The tent *had* been hot.

"I have to go find your brother," Mom said to Jean, "but why don't you and Dad get a drink?"

"That's a great idea," Dad said. "Come on, Jean—we'll get some thistleberry tea to wash that nasty liver taste out of our mouths!"

Magnus looked scandalized. "Excuse me, Professor Huddy," he said, "but *some* of us take the Tasting of the Sacred Bear Liver very seriously. If I had been of age to take part this year, I surely wouldn't be complaining about the taste."

Jean believed him. Magnus had missed being old enough to participate in this year's tasting by only three weeks, and he'd been grumping about it for ages.

"Well, good for you," Dad said. "Now, if you'll excuse me and my daughter . . ."

"I'll join you!" Magnus said heartily. "A cup of thistleberry tea sounds like just the thing to quaff in this weather. *Q-U-A-F-F*—it means 'to drink.'" Since he'd won the bee, Magnus was constantly spelling and defining words.

"And then," he continued, "we can all head to town hall for my father's Founders' Day address."

The mayor's address! Jean sighed, though she tried to direct her breath away from Magnus, sure it still smelled like liver-vomit. Mayor King was known for his endless, droning speeches. And considering that he was running for reelection *and* had a proposal up for a vote next week, his speech tonight was likely to be longer than most.

Magnus fell into step beside Jean and her dad—no escaping him now.

Festival activities were resuming around the square: Brass instruments echoed from the band shell, and children shrieked as they chased each other, waving toy harpoons they'd won at a game booth. Food carts switched on their lamps as the weak arctic sun sank over the fjord-waters. Jean looked around for Katrin but couldn't find her in the crowd.

Dad steered them to the thistleberry tea cart, and Magnus stepped right up. "Three mugs," he said to the vendor. "For me and the Huddys—my treat."

The vendor frowned slightly, and Jean didn't blame him. "My treat," coming from a King, really meant it would be the vendor's treat, since the mayor's family was never actually made to pay for anything in St. Polonius. She turned to

Dad to protest, but he had fallen into conversation with Pastor Thornhill in line behind them.

"Would you get a load of that?" Magnus said as he passed Jean a mug. "The Ratanas are here." Their classmate Isara Ratana and his parents were leaving the performance tent. Like Jean, Isara wore a red bracelet that meant he was old enough to taste the Sacred Bear Liver.

The Ratanas had moved to town the year before, all the way from Thailand. Isara's parents had opened a restaurant called the Tasty Thai Hut that Jean had never tried but Katrin said was good. Isara was fairly quiet at school. When he did speak, he had a bit of an accent, but he had mastered their language speedily; in fact, he had long outlasted Jean in the spelling bee.

"Why wouldn't they be here?" Jean asked.

"Well . . . because they aren't *from* here." Magnus spoke slowly, like he was back at the bee, spelling out a complicated word for the judges. "Founders' Day is for St. Polonians, to celebrate *our* history."

Jean didn't like what he was getting at. "There are plenty of people who live in this town but aren't from here," she said. "Like Katrin's mom . . . and my dad's neighbor at the university, Dr. Fields. No one complains about *them* participating."

"That's different," Magnus said. "Dr. Fields is from Bigsby, right on the other side of the fjord. And Katrin's mom moved here decades ago. The Ratanas haven't even been here a year!"

Jean took a swig of her thistleberry tea, letting its warm sweet-and-sourness roll around her mouth. She was pretty sure the real reason Magnus didn't like the Ratanas was that before they'd arrived, he'd been the best soccer player on the primary school's team. Now Isara was the champ.

Magnus rubbed his medal against his coat, ridding it of snowflakes. "We'd better head inside," he said, "if we want to nab good spots for my father's address. It was *my* idea to hold it in town hall this year—so everyone can listen comfortably to the entire speech, protected from the elements."

And so no one can escape, Jean thought glumly.

Magnus cleared his throat and offered Jean his arm. "Ms. Huddy, may I escort you? There's something I'd like to ask you about along the way."

Jean nearly choked on her tea. Why was Magnus taking an interest in her all of a sudden? She was glad Katrin wasn't around to see, or she'd never hear the end of it. It was bad enough that this was happening in front of her dad.

Dad, though, looked amused. "What a *great* idea!" he said. "Yes, let's go get the best seats in the house!" He swung his hand out in enthusiasm—and dumped his mug of tea all over his pants.

"Oh!" he cried, though he didn't sound upset. "How clumsy of me. I think I've got extra pants in the truck. Jean, will you help me find them?"

As what Dad was doing dawned on her, Jean could hardly suppress a grin. "Yes," she said, trying not to sound too chipper. "Of course I will. Well, good Founders' Day, Magnus."

"Er—good Founders' Day," Magnus echoed, but Dad had grabbed Jean's mittened hand and was already pulling her away.

It wasn't until they were at the other end of the square that Jean dared to speak again. "Dad. That wasn't an accident, was it?"

Snowflakes twinkled on Dad's eyelashes. "Of course not," he said. "And I haven't got any spare clothes. But one pair of wet pants is a small price to pay to skip that speech, don't you think? Now come on—your mom and Micah are meeting us at the truck."

ST. POLONIUS-ON-THE-FJORD
MUST MODERNIZE!

IMAGINE

CELL PHONE COVERAGE ALL OVER TOWN!

RELIABLE SATELLITE TELEVISION AND INTERNET THROUGHOUT THE YEAR!

AN ECONOMY THAT DOES NOT RELY ON THE WHIMS OF TOURISTS!

ALL THIS CAN BE ACCOMPLISHED USING OUR NATIVE NORTHERN FRUIT!

A STATE-OF-THE-ART THISTLEBERRY PROCESSING PLANT IS THE ANSWER!
VOTE YES ON OCTOBER 21

Paid for by the Campaign to Reelect Mayor Theobald King
with additional support from the National Thistleberry Council

CHAPTER 2

“That fool mayor can speechify all he wants,” Mom said as she piloted their ancient truck onto the east road. “But he’s not changing my vote. Besides, the snow’s getting heavier, and our roast is waiting at home.”

Jean stared out the window. The snow *was* falling thickly, and it was a long drive back to the family’s sheep farm on the outskirts of town. But she couldn’t help wondering if her parents had hustled them away to get her as far as possible from the mess she'd made behind the performance tent.

At least Micah didn't seem to know what she'd done. He'd hardly stopped talking about the play since they'd gotten in the car.

"Hey, Jeannie, did you see the part when I twisted the cutlass in the bear's gut?"

"Yes, it—"

"And the part where I passed chunks of his bloody liver around to all the other sailors?"

"Yes, you—"

"And the part where I fell to my knees and cried out 'O, ye sweet saints, take mercy on a poor band o' wayward mariners—' "

This time, Dad cut in. "Micah, man, you were absolutely terrific, but we could use a little quiet. Mom and I are having a serious talk about politics."

Micah sulked at this, but Jean leaned forward in her seat. Maybe if she asked a few intelligent questions about the election, it would help make up for her earlier failure.

The speech they had skipped out on was sure to focus on the mayor's pet project: building a thistleberry processing plant in the town. The plant would turn the area's native thistleberries into products like candies and smoothie mixes. But Mayor King hadn't quite convinced the townspeople that this was a good idea, and his arguments were getting desperate.

The windshield wipers squeaked and grumbled against the building snow. "The numbers are close," Mom said.

“Did you see the latest poll in the *St. Polonius Spyglass*? Fifty-two percent against the thistleberry plant. This may be the first time a mayor’s proposal has failed.”

“King must have something up his sleeve, though,” Dad said. “We know he’s in cahoots with the National Thistleberry Council.”

Mom rolled her window down and spat out of it. “I never thought I’d see the day when outside influences played a part in a St. Polonian election!”

“Mom, it’s freezing back here,” Micah complained. “The snow’s coming in!”

“Sorry, kiddo.” She cranked the window back into place.

“Well, I heard he’s got a chunk of the King family fortune invested in the plant,” Dad said. “If the measure doesn’t pass, the Kings could lose quite a bit.”

This seemed like a good moment to jump in. “What would be so bad about building a thistleberry plant?” Jean asked.

“What would be so bad about building a thistleberry plant?!” her parents cried.

Great—now Jean looked even stupider than before. "Er," she said, "it's just that everyone's always complaining about how bad the TV and Internet and cell phone coverage are here. I mean, we can't even make calls other than local land-line ones in the winter! Didn't that last flyer say we could get better satellite service with money from thistleberry products?"

"This is about far more than upgrading a few satellites, Jean," Mom explained. "In St. Polonius, our professions have been in our families for centuries—ever since the first sailors landed. We take pride in our skills. And no one wants to give up their family trade to work in a factory, not even for more money."

"Plus, if the plant gets built," Dad added, "all the adults in this town will have to take shifts there to keep the production running. How would we find enough time for our own work?"

Jean thought of Dad's books and Mom's sheep. Who would tend to them if they had to go off to work in a factory?

"Okay," she murmured, "I get it." But maybe there was another way to raise money? Year-round TV and Internet sure would make the dreary cold months go by a lot faster. Once the cloud cover set in over St. Polonius for the long winter, their old satellites didn't work at all.

"That ridiculously outdated town charter is part of the problem, too," Mom added as the truck took a slippery turn. "It gives the mayor far too much power over the fate of this town. What we *need* is a fairly elected council that can examine and reform it. If I had my way . . ."

She continued until the truck bounced down their long, snow-packed driveway and into the shed.

"Feast!" Micah cried, leaping out and racing for the house. For Founders' Day, Mom had slow-roasted a leg of lamb all afternoon in the oven. Jean always marveled at how Micah—who claimed to love the family's flock of sheep more than anything else in the world—also seemed to love the taste of lamb more than anything else in the world.

In the kitchen, the aroma of the roast mingled with the scents of honey-baked root vegetables, garlicky mustard greens, buckwheat biscuits, and the condiment that graced every table in St. Polonius: sweet thistleberry relish.

Ten minutes later, the table was laid with the holiday china, silver, and lacy napkins, and Mom had reheated the side dishes. Dad had changed out of his tea-stained pants, and Micah had changed out of his costume.

Mom returned to the kitchen to put the finishing touches on the roast while Dad unfolded his napkin in his lap. "Great saints, but I am sleepy," he said, repeating Cora Buggins's line in the play with an exaggerated yawn. "Maybe I'm getting too old for all this Founders' Day fun." He put an elbow on the table, rested his chin in his hand, and closed his eyes.

Micah laughed, and Jean reached her foot out to give Dad's leg a playful nudge. "Our dad, too old for fun?" she said. "Never!"

But instead of nudging her back, Dad collapsed face-first into a bowl of parsnips.

CHAPTER 3

"Dad?"

Jean and Micah both jumped up. "Dad!" Jean cried again. "Are you okay?"

He didn't answer. She and Micah raced to his side. They pulled his face out of the dish and shook his shoulders. His fall had upset the mustard greens and thistleberry relish, and a red stain was spreading over the tablecloth.

A terrific crash sounded from the kitchen.

"Mom?" Micah called. No answer.

Dad's eyes were closed and his cheeks hung slack, but he was still breathing. "Micah, keep trying to wake him up!" Jean cried, and she tore down the hallway. The first thing she saw when she burst into the kitchen was the leg of lamb: it had tumbled from its pan and skidded across the floor, leaving a trail of grease and peppercorns.

Sprawled on the floor a few feet away was Mom.

Jean dropped to Mom's side, grabbing for one of her oven-mitted hands. "Mom? Mom, wake up! Please!"

Jean's heart was a tiny bird, frantically flapping its wings in her throat. But Mom didn't even flutter an eyelash. Dropping the mitt, Jean fumbled for the kitchen phone and stabbed the emergency button that dialed the St. Polonius Clinic.

The line rang once . . . twice . . . three times. That wasn't right. The only other time Jean had had to call it (when he was five, Micah had broken his arm in the sheep paddock), her call had been taken immediately by Mrs. Cornish, one of the ambulance driver-medics. Jean knew Mrs. Cornish, of course, just like she knew the other driver, Mr. Ludavisk. She and Micah knew most of the adults in St. Polonius—it was a very small town.

But no one answered. The helpline was supposed to be staffed at all times. Jean remembered having seen Mr. Ludavisk receiving his scoop of liver earlier that day—he'd taken an extra spoonful for Mrs. Cornish so she wouldn't have to leave her post.

Had whoever was on duty snuck off for a quick slice of thistleberry pie with their family?

On the twelfth ring, Jean hung up. Racking her brain, she tried to remember what Dr. Hammerstein had taught her class about medical emergencies during their school trip to the clinic. A person might pass out if they were choking, if food had blocked off their airway. But in that case, the person would stop breathing and turn blue. Mom's eyes were closed, and her spiky hair stuck out in every direction . . . but her face was still a healthy color.

Jean raced back to the dining room; Dad wasn't blue, either. In fact, he was snoring on the tablecloth, each exhale causing the mustard greens in front of his lips to quiver gently.

Micah stood beside him, quaking. "What's going on?"

"Mom is . . ." Jean paused, but there was no way to shield her brother. "She's passed out. Like Dad."

The color drained from Micah's face.

"I called the emergency line," Jean continued, "but nobody answered."

"What?" Micah cried. "But we're having a *real* emergency!"

"I know!" Jean tried to keep the panic out of her voice, for Micah's sake. She made herself take a deep breath. "Okay, let's—let's call again."

Micah grabbed the phone and punched the emergency button. He listened to the receiver for a few seconds, then passed it to Jean with a stricken look. "It's busy."

"It can't be!" But Jean heard the *beep-beep-beep* of a busy tone.

During Jean's class trip to the clinic, Mrs. Cornish had showed them the emergency switchboard. It had ten different lines so the clinic would never miss a call.

How could there be that many emergencies at once? Jean wondered. St. Polonius-on-the-Fjord had fewer than four hundred residents; it seemed impossible that so many of them would call the helpline at the same time.

Jean hung up. What could have caused Mom and Dad to pass out? Every idea that came to her seemed more outlandish than the last. *Gas leak?* No, that would have knocked her and Micah out, too. *Food poisoning?* Couldn't be—they hadn't even started their dinner. *Stroke?* Maybe . . . but what were the odds that both of your parents would have a stroke at exactly the same moment?

Jean rattled Dad's arm again, but he snored on. Their situation was dire—snow had been falling for hours, and they were five miles from town with no close neighbors. Mom always said that the farm's founders had preferred the company of sheep to people. Jean mentally cursed her antisocial ancestors.

She had to show Micah that someone was still in charge. "We'll lay them down," she said.

"Huh?"

"If Mom and Dad are both sleeping, we should move them somewhere they'll be comfortable . . . you know, so they won't be all achy and sore when they wake up, the way *you* get when you fall asleep in weird places."

Micah nodded. "Where should we put them? Their bedroom?"

Jean shook her head. "We won't be able to lift them up onto the bed. But maybe we can get them in there." She pointed to the living room. "We can make a bed for them on the floor with the couch cushions."

Micah ran to get blankets while Jean set up the cushions. Then they pulled Dad into a sitting position and wiped the parsnips and relish off his face with the lacy napkin that still sat in his lap.

They couldn't pick him up, so they dragged him into the living room still in his chair, then sort of tipped him out onto the cushions, hoping he didn't hit them too hard.

Next, Jean lifted Mom from under her shoulders and Micah took her legs, but they could barely drag-carry her a few feet down the hallway at a time. When they finally got her onto the cushions, their foreheads were damp with sweat.

At least their parents looked peaceful once they'd been tucked in—as though, after a long day of celebrating, they'd decided to take a little nap together on the farmhouse floor. As though they might wake up any moment, refreshed.

The telephone jangled, and Jean lunged for it. Maybe the helpline was calling her back! "Hello?"

"Jean? Is that you?" The line crackled, but Jean recognized Katrin's voice.

Katrin—who lived in town—one block from the clinic! Why hadn't Jean thought of calling her before?

"Katrin, thank goodness!" Jean cried. "Listen, I need you to run to the clinic right away and tell them to send the ambulance out to the farm. We've been calling the emergency line, but we can't get through! It's our parents. They . . . they won't wake up."

Something about saying the words out loud made it all feel too real. Jean waited for Katrin to reply . . . but only a faint buzz sounded through the phone line.

"Katrin?"

A great gust of wind buffeted the farmhouse. There was another burst of static, and the line went dead.

Jean heard a noise outside and turned to see the telephone wire slapping uselessly against the window. "Rotten shark meat!" she cursed.

Micah saw it, too. "The phone wire's busted?"

This happened almost every year during one storm or another, though usually not until much later in the season. "Looks like it," Jean said. "But if Katrin heard what I was saying, she'll send help."

They sat down next to their parents on the floor and waited. Micah was the least wiggly Jean had ever seen him, which only made her more nervous. Time ticked by on the grandfather clock in the corner; every five minutes or so, they would try to rouse their parents.

Thirty minutes passed. Sixty.

"I don't think anyone's coming," Micah said.

Jean hated to admit that she agreed—especially when she noticed tears filling Micah's brown eyes, which were so like their mom's. She scooted closer and put an arm around him. "Hey, it'll be all right. Mom and Dad . . . they're tough, you know?"

Micah sniffled, but nodded.

"We'll stay close to them tonight, and if they don't wake up by morning, we'll go into town ourselves for help."

Micah pulled away and looked at Jean like she was insane. "Go into town? How?"

Jean gazed out the window at the dark sky and blowing snow. "We'll—we'll walk."

"What?" Micah leapt to his feet. "We can't walk all that way! It's five miles!"

Jean steeled her voice. "Of course we can—and anyway, we don't have any other choice. The road's going to be buried too deep for cars. Mom barely got the truck home."

"Maybe we can sled," Micah suggested.

"It's too flat."

"We can get something to pull the sled, then. One of the sheep!"

A recent lesson from science—Jean's best subject at school—made her shake her head. "Not enough surface tension," she said. "A sheep's hooves would sink right into the snow; we'd be stuck before we'd even made it off the property. If we wear snowshoes when we go, though, it'll be fine!" But even as she said this, she thought again. Snowshoeing took a lot of energy, and neither she nor Micah had ever hiked close to five miles in weather like this.

Still, she gave him what she hoped was a reassuring smile. "Speaking of the sheep, why don't we go check on them? We'll make sure they have enough to eat and drink. Mom and Dad'll be all right on their own for a few minutes."

Micah perked up a little. "Okay."

They pulled their boots and coats on and stepped out into the moonlit snow. The tracks their truck had made less than two hours earlier had disappeared.

A chorus of *baaah*s greeted Jean and Micah as they slid open the heavy barn door. The biting chill in the air muted the smells of hay and dung, but the cold didn't seem to have hurt the sheep any. Their automatic feeding system was working as usual, and their water troughs were free of ice, thanks to the farm's geothermal heating system.

Micah paused to scratch his favorite animal, Rambo, between his curly horns. "I guess whatever's wrong with Mom and Dad doesn't affect sheep."

"I guess not," Jean agreed. She reached out to pet a fat ewe. "Ow!"

The ewe had nipped her finger. It wasn't the first time, either—of all the members of the family, the sheep only bit *her.* It was almost like they knew that, even though Jean was destined to inherit the farm one day, deep down she didn't want to become a sheep farmer.

Unfortunately, choosing your own career wasn't possible in St. Polonius-on-the-Fjord—there wouldn't be enough people to work all the essential jobs if everyone got to do what they liked. Each generation produced a few rebels, of course, who ran off to seek their fortunes and left their families' businesses to collapse. Once they left, no one ever mentioned their names again.

Micah had crouched beside Rambo to examine one of his hooves.

"Is something wrong with him?" Jean asked.

"Oh, no—he's fine."

"Good. Then we should probably head back."

But Micah leaned in closer to the ram. "I want to stay here a little longer," he said. "I'll be in soon, okay?"

"Oh. Sure." Jean forced herself to turn back toward the barn door alone. As much as she wanted to keep Micah close, she shouldn't insist he come straight in; seeing their parents comatose had to be even more upsetting for him than it was for her. A few more minutes with the sheep would probably be good for him. Wasn't that what people who liked animals said about spending time with them?

Jean hurried back to the house and knelt beside her parents again. "Mom? Dad?" They slept on, still breathing. Motionless.

Her parents' cheeks were rosy; they didn't look ill. Jean leaned in closer, and the red bracelet she'd received at the festival slid down her wrist.

Then, like the tentacles of an arctic squid, a terrible thought wrapped itself around her brain. What if her parents weren't sick at all? What if they'd been punished . . . by the saints?

Because she'd thrown up her liver? Could the saints have skipped over her and gone straight to cursing the people she loved?

Codwash, Mom would say. *Superstitions and nonsense.*

But Mom wasn't awake to say those things now. "Codwash," Jean tried, but her voice sounded pathetic—kind of like Mayor King's the day he'd stopped by last summer. He'd sat right here and tried to convince Mom to plow up one of her sheep-grazing pastures and plant thistleberry bushes instead. Mom had just about laughed him off the property.

Would she ever laugh like that again?

Jean pushed herself to her feet, eager to start something—anything—that would distract her. She cleared the dining room table, put things in the refrigerator, and rescued the remains of the lamb roast, slicing away the part that had hit the floor.

She wasn't hungry, but she toasted a buckwheat biscuit anyway and spread it with thistleberry jam; then she carried her plate to the living room and climbed onto the now-cushionless couch. Springs dug into her bottom, but she stayed where she was, gazing down at her parents' placid faces while she ate. Maybe by some miracle, they'd be awake by the time she finished.

Shut your eyes, sleepy little one,
The codfish are slumb'ring in the sea;
The whales do not crest,
The Kraken's at rest,
The shrimp are all dreaming shrimp dreams. . . .
–traditional St. Polonian lullaby

CHAPTER 4

Jean didn't remember falling asleep. She only knew that, suddenly, faint sunlight was glowing through the frosted window and her backside felt like it had been branded with a couch-spring-shaped iron. As she leapt up, last night's plate thudded from her lap to the carpet.

"Mom? Dad? Micah!"

Nobody answered. She looked down; her parents were still in their floor-bed, sleeping soundly.

But where was her brother?

Jean stumbled down the hallway to Micah's bedroom. A mess, as usual—except for the bed, which was still made up.

He hadn't slept in his bed last night.

"Micah!" Jean ran to the bathroom, then the kitchen. "Micah!"

He wasn't in the house. A balloon of anxiety expanded in her chest. Micah had that amazing ability to fall asleep almost anywhere—but he couldn't have gone to sleep in the barn, could he? The sheep, with their warm layers of wool, could stand the nighttime temperature dips, but a skinny boy of eight was another story. Jean had felt cold after only ten minutes in the barn last night, wearing snow pants and a coat. She pulled those layers back on.

As she yanked her knee-high boots on with shaking hands, an even worse thought crossed her mind: what if her parents' mysterious sleeping condition had struck Micah out in the barn? She pictured him keeling over with his mittens off, right in the middle of examining Rambo's hoof . . . then imagined his fingers all puffed up and red with frostbite.

How could she have left him out there on his own?

Jean barreled out the door, stumbled into a waist-high snowdrift, righted herself, and pushed on toward the barn. The snow was two feet high in the shallowest spots, nearly three feet in others, and still sprinkling down. There was no way she'd be able to hike to town in these conditions—and if Micah was hurt, she needed help more than ever.

Jean wrenched the barn door open. "Micah!" Her voice

echoed off the barn's walls, then the sound of *baaah*ing filled her ears. She started to run up and down the rows of pens, but when she reached Rambo's, she stopped short. There was her brother, on his knees by the edge of the enclosure, in the same position she'd left him in last night.

Frozen in place?

"Micah!"

He turned toward her. His face was drawn and gray, with bags under his bloodshot brown eyes. But he was smiling. "Jeannie!"

She practically collapsed on top of him as she hugged him. "I was so worried," she murmured. Once he'd wriggled free, she yanked off her mittens and grabbed his bare hands in her own. They were cold, but not frozen.

"Sorry I scared you," he said, "but hey, come look at these! I've been up all night working on them."

He pointed into Rambo's pen. Wrapped around each of the ram's four hooves was a kind of bootie that flattened out at the bottom, where it attached to something that looked like a small tennis racket.

"They're snowshoes!" Micah announced proudly. "For Rambo—so he can pull our sled into town without sinking into the snow!"

At that moment, Rambo took an awkward step, and the strange new weight of the snowshoe on his hoof made him stumble forward with a *clonk*.

"They'll work better once he's outside," Micah said. "I think."

Jean could hardly believe her eyes. She knew Micah

was creative, but this! "You made snowshoes for a sheep? How?"

Micah pointed to their mom's work area. "Mom's supplies—wood and other things."

Jean nodded—though as the older sister, it really should have been *her* inventing a brilliant plan to get them into town while her brother slept.

"The snowshoes look great," she said.

Micah broke into a fresh smile. "Thanks." He reached into the pen to help Rambo back up into a standing position. "Mom and Dad didn't wake up in the night, did they?"

Jean shook her head. "We'll have to head to town. But first, breakfast."

Once they'd devoured the leftover biscuits and all the yogurt in the refrigerator, they were outside the barn, ready to go. They had left a note right on top of their parents' quilt (*Dear Mom and Dad, We went to town to find help for you. Love, Jean and Micah*), and Jean had used rope to rig Rambo up to their best wooden sled.

She climbed into the back of the contraption, and Micah squeezed in in front of her. It was tight—the sled was only supposed to carry one person at a time. But together, they'd stay warmer. Through the eye-holes in her balaclava, Jean could see that the snow was starting to come down harder again. There were already ice crystals forming in Rambo's wool, and he'd been outside for only a few minutes.

Micah snapped the rope-reins, and over the sound of the wind, he yelled, "Giddyap!"

Rambo didn't move.

"Giddyap! Go, Rambo, you glorious sheep!"

That seemed to do it. Rambo took one tentative step forward, then another. The shoes Micah had made kept him from sinking too deep into the snow, and after a few jerky lurches, their sled began to move toward the road.

"Woo-hoo!" Micah whooped. "Good boy! To town!"

But Rambo didn't know which way town was; he'd never been farther than the edge of the pasture. Every two or three minutes, Micah or Jean had to jump out of the sled and slog through waist-high snow to push Rambo in the right direction. It took them nearly twenty minutes to get out to the road, normally a five-minute walk.

"Are you sure this is a good idea?" Jean shouted as Micah climbed back in after pulling Rambo through the front gate. "I don't think he's saving us any time!"

"It'll be better once we're off the property!" Micah shouted back. "Then he can follow the road!"

But half an hour later, even Micah had to admit he'd been wrong. Rambo seemed happy to walk in zigzags or circles while the wind sent sheets of snow crashing into their sled like frozen ocean waves.

Soon Jean's balaclava was crusted over with ice, and Micah looked like a miniature abominable snowman. She tapped him on his shoulder, then poked him, but he was wearing too many layers to feel it. She finally had to punch him to get his attention. He turned his head as far toward her as he could.

"We need," she cried, "to turn ba—"

A gust of snow blew into their faces, and Rambo stopped in his tracks.

"Hey!" Micah yelled. "What's that noise?"

A low, rumbling sound. Getting louder, fast.

Something came into view up ahead on the road, and Jean stood on the back of the sled to see better. Headlights cast two sharp beams through the snowflakes.

"Look!" she shrieked. She yanked Micah to his feet. "The snowplow!"

Micah punched a mittened fist in the air. "It's Mr. Gorson! Axel's dad!"

Mr. Gorson, the snowplow driver, was opening up the road. He would take them into town, where they would get Dr. Hammerstein and race back to the farm to cure their parents of their mysterious illness. *It has to be an illness,* Jean told herself, *not a curse.* They'd be awake and eating leftover lamb by sunset.

Jean and Micah waved to hail the plow. It was shoving huge quantities of snow off the road, fast. Odd; Mr. Gorson was usually fussy about his work. "If that man plowed the roads any more slowly," Dad liked to complain, "we'd be stuck out at the farm from Founders' Day to Christmas."

Maybe Mr. Gorson knew that this was an emergency. Or maybe . . .

Jean squinted at the truck's cab as Micah shouted, "Jean! That's not Mr. Gorson!"

The person in the driver's seat didn't have the chief

plowman's thick gray beard or tall, sloping forehead; in fact, he was barely tall enough to see over the dashboard.

Eight-year-old Axel Gorson was behind the wheel of his dad's two-ton snowplow—and it was barreling, at top speed, straight toward them.

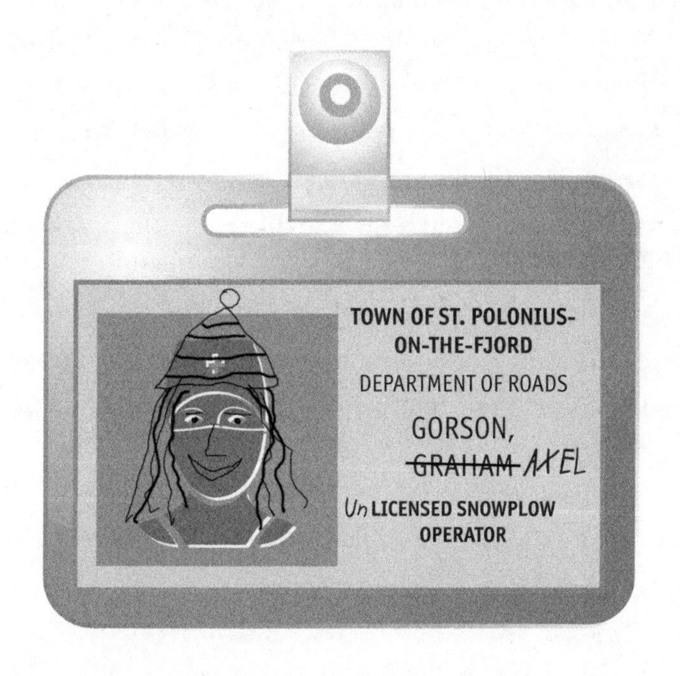

CHAPTER 5

"DIVE!"

Jean grabbed her brother around the waist and leapt. They landed face-first in a drift, and Jean scrambled to find Micah's arm and pull him out of the snowplow's path. Rambo clomped across the road, ropes trailing behind him.

The truck's brakes squealed—too late. It ran right over

Jean and Micah's best sled with a loud, splintery *crunch* before skidding to a stop, front plow jammed into a snowbank.

Ice had scraped the skin around Jean's eyes, and it stung as she tore off her balaclava. "Micah? Are you okay?"

Snow fell from Micah's hood as he nodded. "Rambo?"

Jean pointed across the road. Rambo was nosing into a snow-coated evergreen bush, searching for a snack as though nothing had happened. "Good boy," Micah said.

Axel jumped down from the cab. He wore his dad's Roads Department uniform, though the red jacket was enormous on him, and Mr. Gorson's green snow boots came up to his thighs.

"Oi, farm-dwellers!" he shouted. His long brown hair whipped wildly around his head in the wind. "I've come to rescue you! You're welcome in advance!"

"Rescue?" Micah's face was thistleberry-red. "You almost ran over me, and my sister, and my sheep!" He and Jean advanced along the freshly plowed road toward Axel. "Why are you even driving this thing, anyway? Your dad's gonna kill you!"

Axel, shielding his face from the falling snow, squinted at them. "He's not gonna find out."

"Oh yes he is," Micah shouted. "I'll tell him myself!"

"You'll have to wake him up first!"

Jean froze. *Wake him up?* "Axel . . . what are you talking about?"

Axel suddenly seemed a little smaller. "It happened l-last night," he said, his teeth starting to chatter. "And not just to my dad. All the adults, and the teenagers—they dropped like snowflies. There was nothing we could do to stop it."

"*Everybody's* asleep? What's going on, Jeannie?" Micah turned to his sister, his eyes round. Jean tensed. Was the whole town sick?

Or worse—cursed?

"I don't know what's happening," she murmured. "But it doesn't sound good."

"Look, can we all talk in the truck?" Axel asked. "I'm turning into an icicle!"

Micah elbowed Jean. "What about Rambo?"

In the time they'd been standing with Axel, Rambo had moved several yards farther down the road. *Of course he'd pick now to start going in the right direction,* Jean thought. "Get him, I guess."

While Micah trudged off to wrangle his sheep, Jean followed Axel to the truck. He'd left the engine running, and heat blasted her face when she climbed into the cab. She scooted into the middle seat, tugged off her mittens, and stretched her numb fingers out over the vent. "Sweet St. Polonius," she breathed, "that feels good."

A minute later the passenger door opened, and Micah tried to coax Rambo up into the truck. Rambo was having none of it.

"Hurry up," Axel moaned. "You're letting all the heat out!"

"Hang on." After another minute of rope-yanking and baaing, Rambo was finally wedged in at Micah's feet, and Micah was next to Jean.

"Hey, what's that?" Axel pointed to the long slab of wood that Micah had carried into the cab.

Jean felt Micah stiffen. "What's left of our sled, thanks to you."

"Lemme see." Axel leaned across Jean and yanked the slab out of Micah's hand.

"Hey!" Micah cried, but Axel stuck the slab between his knees and used it to poke the gas pedal. The engine revved.

"Perfect," he said. He then pulled out what looked like a thick tree branch and tossed it out of the truck.

"You've been using a *branch* to reach the pedals?" Jean asked.

"Yep," Axel said, "but I think this piece of sled'll work much better. Okay, ready to go?" He reached for the gear-shift, but Jean grabbed it first.

"No way," she said. "You're not driving us anywhere—we just came in here to talk."

"I can talk and drive at the same time," Axel said.

"I doubt it," Micah muttered.

If Axel heard this insult, he ignored it. "Look, if you want to make it into town for the big meeting," he said, "the Axel-Taxi's the only way."

Jean's hand stayed on the gearshift. "What meeting?"

"The one Magnus King has called—at the school-house at noon. Which is"—Axel checked the clock on the dashboard—"seven minutes from now. We're gonna have to drive fast!"

"No *way,*" Jean said.

Axel groaned. "But he's gonna read from the St. Polonius

town charter! He says it has instructions for how to deal with a . . . a . . . a *crisis* like this one." Axel's gray eyes narrowed. "Don't you want to find out how to wake up your parents?"

Jean's heart panged. Of *course* she wanted to wake her parents, but she needed more information. "Let's go back to the beginning," she said. "What, exactly, happened last night in town?"

"It started a few minutes into the mayor's speech at town hall," Axel said. "He kept talking about how great a thistle-berry plant would be, and how everyone needed to vote for it, and at first I thought people were falling asleep 'cause it was boring, ya know? But then my dad slid right out of his chair and onto the floor, and when I tried to wake him up, I couldn't." Axel gulped. "It was horrible."

Jean pictured the scene: adults fainting right and left, kids panicking. She squeezed her brother's mitten, and he squeezed back.

"What did you do?" she asked Axel.

"Well, me and a couple of other kids ran to the health clinic," he said. "We thought they might be able to figure out what was going on. But when we got there, Mrs. Cornish was already collapsed at the switchboard, and Dr. Hammerstein was asleep on one of her exam tables."

Jean nodded slowly. That was why she and Micah hadn't been able to reach anyone on the emergency helpline.

"So then what?" Micah asked.

"Everyone was freaking out," Axel continued. "Some kids thought their parents were *dead*! Even the mayor had passed out behind his podium. It was Magnus who calmed everyone down. He got up onstage and showed us that his dad was still breathing. Then he organized everyone to fold up the chairs and put them away so the sleepers would have more room to stretch out on the floor. And he called today's meeting so everyone who was left awake could come find out what to do."

"And the only people left awake are . . . kids?" Jean asked.

Axel nodded. "Yeah. I don't think I saw anyone still awake who was older than you, Jean."

Jean's grip on the gearshift slackened. It sounded like Magnus had actually done a good job taking charge of things. And she supposed that if anyone was going to have access to emergency instructions—like how to call for help in the middle of a blizzard when the mountain pass out of town was closed and the satellites were blocked—it would be the mayor's son.

In the few minutes they'd been talking, snow had blanketed the truck's windshield, blocking any view of the road, trees, or sky. The cab felt close and hot.

"If we let you drive us to this meeting," Jean said, "will you *promise* to be careful? A lot more careful than you were on the drive out here?"

"Of course!" The long red sleeve of his dad's jacket slid up Axel's arm as he raised his right hand. "I swear it on the grave of St. Polonius himself."

Jean nodded; if there was one thing people took seriously in St. Polonius-on-the-Fjord, it was their patron saint. As

Axel flicked on the windshield wipers, Jean checked Micah's seat belt, then let go of the gearshift.

"All right. Drive us into town."

"Yee-haw!" Axel shoved the gearshift into reverse, slammed on the gas with his sled-slab, and yanked the steering wheel like it was a bear he was wrestling for his life. The truck spun, throwing everyone to the right. Rambo let out a panicked *BAAAH!*

"Hey!" Jean cried, but Axel—a maniacal grin plastered across his face—didn't seem to hear as he jammed the gas again and sent them racing toward town. Trees whipped by at a frightening pace, dumping their powdery loads onto the windshield when the snowplow clipped their branches.

"AXEL!" Jean yelled. "SLOW *DOWN*!" She was sure he had heard her. But instead of hitting the brake, he lifted his hands off the steering wheel and let out a wild whoop.

The truck hit an icy bump and launched into the air.

Jean threw an arm across Micah's chest and closed her eyes. This was it. They were all going to die.

The truck seemed airborne for an eternity before it hit the road with a string of jarring bounces. Another terrified *BAAAH!* rose from the floor, and Jean's brains felt like scrambled goose eggs. But they were still alive—and the truck was still going.

"Atta plow!" Axel shouted, slapping the steering wheel.

Jean considered choking him—his scrawny neck was in easy reach. But they were still miles from town, from help. She stuffed her hands back into their mittens, sat on them, and prayed to all the saints she wasn't sure she believed in that they would get to the schoolhouse in one piece.

They shot past a sign:

WELCOME TO ST. POLONIUS-ON-THE-FJORD, EST. 1674
A LOVELY HAMLET IN WHICH TO LIVE!

Cottages belonging to shopkeepers, fisherfolk, and town employees like Mr. Gorson began to appear. Simple homes with thick walls to keep out the northern winds—one story, a chimney, maybe a goose coop in the yard. No one in St. Polonius had the money to live grandly (except for the Kings; generations of holding the mayorship and never paying for anything had helped them grow rich). But it was a mark of pride for St. Polonians that they didn't need extravagant houses. The dramatic Fortinbras mountain range sat behind them, and the vast North Sea lapped at their doorsteps. Even if people sometimes wanted jobs that didn't exist in St. Polonius, Jean didn't know how they could bring themselves to leave this beautiful place.

Axel swiveled the steering wheel as they entered downtown. It looked deserted, though the truck was streaking down Main Street so fast that Jean wasn't sure she'd be able to spot people if they were there.

"Axel!" she shouted again. "Start slowing down!"

"Oh—right!"

He shifted the slab of wood from the gas pedal to the brake, and the truck began to fishtail down the icy street.

Jean, Micah, and Rambo all screamed as Axel spun the steering wheel left and right, trying to regain control. They jumped the curb in front of the schoolhouse and finally came to a stop in the playground, though not before half an icy teeter-totter had landed in the cradle of the truck's plow.

"Oops." Axel shrugged and undid his seat belt.

Jean wanted to tear out every one of his long hairs. "You promised to drive carefully! You *swore* it on the grave of St. Polonius himself!"

"Yeahhh . . . but St. Polonius doesn't *have* a grave. He was buried at sea, remember?"

Axel leapt out of the truck as Jean lunged. *I'll kill him later,* she thought.

"Jean!" Katrin Ash tugged at the passenger door. "Jean! Micah! You're here!"

Katrin's mom owned the local hair salon and tattoo parlor, and over the last year Katrin had spent countless hours perfecting her punk look. But today . . . well, she looked like something the dogfish had dragged in. Her eyes, normally black-lined, had nothing but bags underneath them, and her hair, usually teased to perfection, was a marmot's nest of snowflake-catching tangles.

"I've been watching out for you guys for ages!" she cried. "What took you so long? I told Axel to drive fast!"

"Yeah, thanks for that," Micah grumbled as he unlocked his seat belt.

Katrin reached up to help him climb out of the cab.

"The meeting's already started. Hurry." She noticed Rambo. "Holy haddock, there's a sheep!"

Rambo stumbled out of the cab and let out a low moan; a string of regurgitated bush needles dribbled from his mouth.

"Ew!" Katrin's platform combat boots stomped back several steps. "Why on earth did you bring this animal with you?"

Micah shot her a loathsome look as he patted Rambo. "Don't listen to her, boy."

Katrin's gaze darted back and forth between Micah and Rambo, like she couldn't decide which one of them was crazier. Finally, shaking her head, she reached up to help Jean down from the truck. "You can explain everything later. Let's get inside."

CHARTER
OF THE
TOWNE OF
ST. POLONIUS-ON-THE-FJORD

Scriven'd by the followers of
CAPTAIN POLONIUS JONES
in the year of our Lord, 1675

Section 1. Be it agreed by all good fellows assembled that this bleak corner of the earth, formerly incapable of supporting human life, hereafter be known as "St. Polonius-on-the-Fjord" in honor of the Sainted Captain Polonius Jones, who by his own hand did miraculously save all forty-two crew members of *The Jolly Narwhal* from certain death through the great miracle of hibernation.

CHAPTER 6

The moment they walked in, a schoolhouse full of heads swiveled in their direction.

About a hundred kids filled the room, grouped by family, babies and toddlers in the arms of older siblings or neighbors. There were the five black-haired heads of the Hansen kids, ages two to eleven, sitting with their cousins, the Petersons. Behind them, the three red heads of the Daly family, who were related to the Hansens, too. Jean and Micah were rare cousinless St. Polonians, since both of their parents were only children.

Closer to the front sat the two younger Marx kids, but their teenage sister was missing. Jean scanned the room: no teenagers at all.

Most of the kids looked like they hadn't gotten a wink of sleep—or had a chance to change out of their Founders' Day clothes. Micah's classmates still wore their sailor costumes; Cora Buggins rocked back and forth on a chair nearby, her eyes glassy as she chewed on the tip of her stuffed narwhal's horn.

But Magnus stood behind a lectern at the front, hair tidy, clothes clean and pressed. His medal was bright, but the look he was giving Jean was as dark as could be.

She swallowed. It wasn't like she'd expected Magnus to dance down the aisle and welcome her—but how about a *little* enthusiasm over seeing the Huddy kids alive? Was he annoyed because her family had skipped out on the mayor's speech the night before?

"Look!" Cora Buggins perked up. "Micah brought a sheep!"

Rambo had finally worked up the courage to poke his head around Micah's leg, but at the excited rumble that went through the crowd, he backed away quickly.

"I'll go stick him in the coat room," Micah said. "Maybe he'll feel better with all that wool around."

Magnus's surly expression vanished as though he had flipped a switch; maybe it was the sheep he had objected to. "Greetings, greetings!" he cried, smiling widely. "Jean—we're so glad you and Micah are here. Come, there's a spot for you right up front. You, too, Katrin."

Jean glanced at Katrin, who shrugged. They were usually more back-row kinds of girls—Jean because she didn't like people staring at her, and Katrin because she liked to whisper snarky comments about whoever was at the front of the room to Jean. But today, Jean supposed, they could make an exception.

Magnus wasn't alone at the lectern. Flanking him were *his* cousins, Bertha and Bartleby Smuthers, better known as B&B. Like Magnus, they had gold glinting at their chests. Not spelling-bee medals, though—St. Polonius police badges.

B&B were twins, and their mother was Constable Eileen Smuthers, the mayor's sister and St. Polonius's one full-time officer of the law. Constable Eileen loved handing out parking tickets.

Her children were much worse.

Rumor had it that B&B had bullied enough pocket money off younger students in the last three years to buy their family a vacation bungalow on the southern coast. Jean didn't believe this (at most, she thought, they'd stolen enough to buy a used camper-van), but she still tried to keep her distance. And even though they were his relatives, straight-arrow Magnus usually did, too. So what were they doing up there?

"Looks like B&B wasted no time raiding their mom's uniform drawer," Katrin whispered. "Ugh. Have a little class."

Magnus tapped his medal against the lectern. "Ladies and gentlemen, please settle down! I am going to read from the town charter." He leaned in over a dusty sheaf of papers.

"It is hereby decreed that, in the instance of incapacitation of an adult citizen of the municipality's population-at-large, that citizen's eldest progeny of the same gender shall subsequently be recruited to fulfill the occupational and civic duties of that citizen until such time as the adult citizen has recovered."

Magnus looked up. "So there we have it. Exact instructions on what to do in a situation like the one we're currently facing."

"Huh?" a voice called. Jean was glad someone had spoken up. She'd hardly understood a word, and judging from all the other blank faces, neither had anyone else.

Magnus's sigh reverberated through his microphone. "In short, the charter says that if an adult is incapacitated—*I-N-C-A-P-A-C-I-T-A-T-E-D,* meaning they can't do their job—their kids are supposed to do it for them until they can work again. So oldest daughters should take over their mothers' jobs, and oldest sons should take over their fathers'."

A murmur rippled through the audience. *This* was the plan?

Katrin jumped to her feet. "Is that really what it says? Let me have a look."

She was halfway to the lectern when Bartleby Smuthers stepped in front of her. "In the name of security," he barked, "I'm going to have to ask you to sit back down."

"In the name of . . . what?" Katrin's voice was incredulous. "I'm not gonna shred the papers or anything—I just want to see them." She tried to move around him, but Bartleby was at least twice as broad as she was. When Bertha stepped up, a wall of Smutherses stood between Katrin and the charter.

"Please don't contradict my brother," Bertha said. "We're just protecting the mayor."

"The mayor?" Katrin shook her head. "The mayor's asleep, like all the other adults, and *I'm* one of the oldest people who's still awake. Magnus, tell these goons to get out of my way so I can see the charter."

"Katrin, please have a seat," Magnus said. "Anyone who wants to look at the town charter themselves will be able to make an appointment to do so at my office—after their own workday is finished, of course."

"What the heck are you *talking* about?" Katrin cried. "You don't have an office, and we don't have workdays. What we *do* have is a bunch of adults and teenagers who need our help. I thought this meeting was called so we could figure out how to do that."

"Yeah!" Jean recognized Micah's shout from the back of the room. Other kids joined in.

Magnus's noble brow creased. "Ladies and gentlemen,"

he said, "if you'll all be quiet and *listen,* everything will make perfect sense!"

With a roll of her eyes, Katrin slipped back into her seat.

"Now," Magnus continued, "regarding the fact that the adults and teenagers in this town have fallen asleep—the explanation is quite simple. Think back to yesterday's Founders' Day play. The exact same thing happened to St. Polonius himself, and his entire crew, back in 1674!"

Everyone gasped. "Our parents," one of the Hansen girls said, "went into *hibernation*?"

"Look at the evidence!" Magnus cried. "On the original Founders' Day, the saints put all the sailors into a miraculous sleep to save them from the harsh blizzards of winter. Yesterday was also Founders' Day, and there was also a blizzard. Clearly, the saints have seen fit to work a miracle once more."

The room was positively abuzz. Axel's voice shouted over the noise of the crowd. "But why?" he asked. "Why would the saints do that to my dad?"

"Who are we to interpret the motivations of the saints?" Magnus asked the crowd. "They must have their own reasons for wanting so many of our citizens to sleep through the season. The important thing is that Captain Polonius and his crew woke back up in the spring, good as new, so there's no need to worry. I'm sure the same thing will happen to our sleepers this time around."

It's a miracle—they were really supposed to accept that as an explanation? Jean wanted clear instructions from the town charter that would help them wake their parents, or at least tell them how to reach someone outside town for aid. But Magnus's grand plan was for them all to have faith and wait until the thaw next year.

"Letting this miracle run its course is the only thing we can do," Magnus said. "The pass is snowed under, and the satellites are down for the season. In the future, money from a thistleberry processing plant could help us upgrade those satellites . . . but for now, unfortunately, we have no way of contacting the outside world for help." Magnus stood up straighter. "So we'll follow the charter and keep St. Polonius running until our parents wake up. This means that school will be suspended. And it also means that you, Katrin Ash, are now the sole proprietor of Ash Beauty and Tattoo Parlor; that Axel Gorson over there is the approved snowplow operator for the St. Polonius Department of Roads; and that I, Magnus King, as the only child of our esteemed elected leader, must now officially take on the role of mayor of St. Polonius-on-the-Fjord."

"All hail Mayor Magnus King!" Bartleby and Bertha cried, snapping their hands to their foreheads in crisp salutes. A few of the younger kids copied them immediately.

Is Magnus bribing B&B to act like this? Jean wondered. They didn't help anyone out—not even family—unless there was something in it for them.

Magnus beamed at his cousins. "Many thanks to our interim police constables," he said, "who were so eager to take on their mother's duties that they offered to join me up here today as my personal bodyguards." He turned his smile back toward the audience. "Now, as for the rest of you, here are the steps you'll need to take to officially assume your par—"

"Wait a minute." The words bubbled out of Jean's mouth before she'd even thought them. Katrin gaped as Jean shuffled to her feet.

Magnus's eyes were on her, along with all of the other eyeballs in the room. Jean didn't like it a bit. "What if it, um, isn't a miraculous hibernation?" she asked, trying to keep her voice steady. "What if everyone is sick—with a disease—and a doctor could help them?"

Magnus's pale eyelashes fluttered. "Are you saying, Jean Huddy, that you think hundreds of people in this town could have all come down with the same illness at the same time? An illness that doesn't affect kids?"

It did sound implausible. But still, what if there was something that everyone who was asleep had done? Or something in common that they all—

"The bear liver!" Jean blurted. "They all ate the Sacred Bear Liver yesterday. Maybe something was wrong with it!"

More gasps rose from the crowd, but Magnus shook his head. "That's preposterous," he said. "Meaning very foolish: *P-R-E-P-O-S-T-E-R-O-U-S*." His eyes locked on Jean's. "You know that the liver is always tested for safety before it's served to the public—your biochemist friend at the university, Dr. Fields, examines it every year. In fact, I was with my father when he brought the liver to her lab, and witnessed the entire thing. And besides," he continued, "our town has been eating bear liver on Founders' Day for centuries, and nothing like this has ever happened since the Founding."

"I didn't mean to insult Dr. Fields," Jean said. Dr. Fields had been a family friend for years; she'd been letting Jean play around—and later, help out—in her lab ever since Jean was a little girl. "I'm just saying that it seems pretty suspicious that everyone who ate the bear liver yesterday is asleep now."

"Yes, everyone who ate it *is* asleep," Magnus pointed out, "except you."

Jean froze.

"So your being awake right now disproves your entire theory, doesn't it?" he asked. "You're of age, you ate the liver yesterday, and you're still awake. Unless . . ." Jean could practically see the wheels in his head turning.

At the back of the room, the door burst open.

"Of course she ate the liver," cried the boy who had just arrived. "She did, and so did I."

Fried Bananas

Ingredients

- Bananas (fresh or frozen)
- Rice flour
- Shredded coconut
- Sugar
- Salt
- Plenty of oil for frying

CHAPTER 7

"Isara!" Katrin whispered as Jean sank back into her seat. "How is he awake?"

Jean shook her head. Isara was thirteen, but all the other teenagers were in hibernation.

"You see!" Magnus cried. "This boy ate the liver, too, and yet here he is, still conscious. So let's forget this liver-sickness idea once and for all. And as for you," he continued, pointing a finger at Isara, "I see that the saints' actions have not affected *your* family. I suppose that they chose to pass you all over, because . . . well, because you aren't true St. Polonians."

This accusation must have stung Isara, but he did a good job of hiding it. "My parents are both asleep at the town hall," he said. "They've been affected as much as everyone else. It's only me who wasn't."

"Oh." Magnus scratched his chin. "Well . . . er . . . then why weren't you here for the beginning of this meeting? I specifically called a meeting for twelve o'clock sharp for *everyone* who was left awake. Do you think you're above the rules of this town?"

"I'm late because I was cooking at our family's restaurant," Isara said. "Since everyone's parents are asleep, I thought the kids might be hungry."

He reached into his satchel and began to pull out small wrapped packages and pass them around. As kids ripped them open, puffs of steam rose from each one.

"Fried bananas!" one of the Daly boys cried. "Thanks, Isara!"

"Thank you, Isara!" the other kids chorused, and a smile crossed Isara's face.

"Wait—stop—" Magnus spluttered. "This snack is not authorized—"

But everyone was too busy eating to listen. When a packet finally landed in her hands, Jean savored its warmth before peeling it open and lifting a slice of crispy, coconut-coated banana to her mouth. It was sweet. In that moment,

Isara probably could have beaten Magnus in a one-on-one race for mayor.

Magnus must have caught on to this, because his switch seemed to flip again. "Good!" he cried. "Yes, enjoy this food, with the mayor's compliments! In fact . . ." He consulted his papers. "Isara Ratana, you are the only child of the owners of the Tasty Thai Hut, correct?"

"I am."

"Excellent," said Magnus. "For the rest of the winter, you will be sole proprietor of the restaurant, in charge of cooking three square meals a day for all the children of this town."

"Um," Isara said, "what?"

Magnus's medal caught a ray of light as he explained the town charter's "plan" for getting them all through the current crisis. "And since the only other restaurant operator in town—Burt Miller, of Ye Olde Mill Inn—has no children," he said, "I'm afraid that the burden of cooking will fall to you alone."

Isara stared up at Magnus. "But the kitchen at my parents' restaurant is very small," he said. "We're used to cooking only a few takeaway orders every night. And we're not even open for breakfast!"

Bartleby Smuthers took a step toward Isara. "Then your hours will have to change, won't they? You'll be open for breakfast tomorrow—or else."

Isara looked at him, puzzled, and Magnus stepped out from behind the lectern to lay a hand on Bartleby's shoulder. "Thank you, Deputy Constable, but there's no need for threats! I'm sure that Isara—and all the other upstanding boys and girls of this town—will be happy to take over their parents' businesses and make adjustments as needed."

"I can't believe this," Katrin whispered to Jean.

"Me either!" Jean turned—and was surprised to see Katrin grinning.

"I've been telling my mom for ages that I'm ready to start cutting hair, but she *never* lets me. Now I'll get a shot at running the business all by myself!"

She was in favor of Magnus's plan?

"Katrin," Jean whispered frantically, "we need to figure out how to *help* our parents, not how to take over their lives while they're sleeping!"

Katrin sighed. "You heard what Magnus said: the pass is closed, the satellites are down. I know you don't want to run your mom's sheep farm, Jean, but what else can we do?"

Jean stared at the ground—she hadn't even considered what her "profession" would be in this new town order. Though as far as the farm went, did she really need to be there? The automatic feeding and watering systems meant the sheep could be fine on their own in the barn for weeks.

"I'm sorry, that was harsh," Katrin whispered. "I just . . . I feel like this could be a big chance for me. You know, to prove myself to my mom."

Looking around the room, Jean could tell Katrin wasn't the only one warming to Magnus's proposal. Cora Buggins's face looked less sad. And Axel Gorson was grinning ear to ear at the prospect of driving his dad's snowplow every day.

"I can't believe I get to take over at the library," said a voice nearby. It belonged to Micah's classmate Eliza

Johanssen, whose parents were the school headmaster and the town librarian. "I've been telling my mom for ages to forget about that old Dewey decimal system. Wait till she wakes up and sees how great the books look grouped by color!"

"And *I* can't wait to start doing operations on people!" replied Dr. Hammerstein's daughter. Annemarie Hammerstein was six.

This was all too much. *What would Mom do?* Jean thought. Before she could lose her nerve, she climbed onto her chair.

"Excuse me!" she shouted. The importance of Jean's mission strengthened her voice. "Excuse me, but I think that we should have a vote."

"A vote?" Bertha Smuthers cried. "A vote on *what*?"

"A vote on whether we think that taking over our parents' jobs is the best course of action, or whether we should do . . . uh, something else. You know . . . find help!"

As her words echoed through the room, Jean realized how lame they sounded. "Wait, I mean—"

But Bartleby was barreling down the aisle toward her. "Get down right now," he snarled. "Get down, or my sister and I will—"

"No, Constables—no," Magnus said. To Jean's surprise, he flashed her a big smile. "Jean is right. Having a vote is an excellent idea."

Jean stared at him. "*You* think so?"

He nodded. "After all, we'll vote again next week, so this will be good practice."

"Vote again?" someone asked.

"Of course," Magnus said. "There's the vote for mayor, and also the vote on my father's proposal to build a thistleberry processing plant. The charter says that children have to take over their parents' 'occupational and civic duties' while they're asleep, and voting is a civic duty."

"So you're saying," Axel called, "that we're all going to vote in our parents' places in the election while they're asleep?"

"Exactly," Magnus said. "That is, assuming the majority here today decides that we should indeed follow the rules set out for our protection in the town charter. All in favor of following Article 205, Clause 44, and keeping this town running in a way that would make our elders proud?"

Up on the chair, Jean watched as nearly every child raised his or her hand—even Katrin, though she mouthed "sorry" to Jean as she did it. Magnus didn't bother to count.

"All opposed?"

Even though it was a lost cause, Jean raised her hand—and gratitude flooded through her when Micah did the same. They were the only ones; even Isara, who looked panicked at the idea of feeding all the kids every day on his own, didn't dare vote against Magnus and the all-powerful charter.

"Then the motion passes!" Magnus thumped the lectern.

Cheers rose, and Jean felt her face glow red as she climbed down. She'd made a fool of herself in front of a large group of people; it was like the spelling bee all over again.

Magnus read out a few more town charter clauses. Mom was right—there were a lot of ridiculous laws still on the books. One said family members were required to take all meals together. Another said town-wide votes must always take place at high noon on the third Saturday of October (as this was the day and time of the very first mayoral election, in 1675). And a related clause said that the results, once cast and counted, were binding for all eternity.

Finally, Magnus instructed everyone to line up at the lectern so he could officially record their job duties and deal with special situations. For instance, anyone under the age of four was excused from work and would go to the local day-care center, and the children of single parents—like B&B—would share their mother's or father's responsibilities among themselves.

Not knowing what else to do, Jean trudged into the line behind Katrin and Isara. But as she waited, her thoughts swam around one point like a shark circling prey. Magnus had said there was no way to contact the outside world for aid—and it was true that the satellites were down and the one road out of town was blocked by snow.

But he *hadn't* mentioned the other settlement that clung to their country's northern shore.

In Jean's mind, a plan was forming—a plan that involved a girl, a boat, and a secret trip across the fjord to the town that was St. Polonius's sworn enemy: Bigsby-on-the-Bay.

CHAPTER 8

"I'm *sorry,*" Katrin said fifteen minutes later, for what seemed like the thousandth time. The meeting had finally ended, and she, Jean, Micah, and Rambo were walking across the snowy playground to her apartment.

Jean was still upset with Katrin for not backing her up in the vote. But she and Micah had no way to get home—not unless they were willing to accept another joyride from Axel.

Jean felt sick at the prospect of leaving her parents alone out on the farm, even though she knew there was nothing she could do for them. At least they were tucked in tight, and the house was warm. The sheep would be fine, too. So when Katrin had invited the Huddy kids to stay with her in town, Jean took it as a peace offering.

"Let's forget about the vote," she said. "It's an ice floe under the bridge, okay?"

Katrin nodded, clearly relieved, and they all turned the corner into the narrow alleyway where she lived.

No trains ran through St. Polonius, but if the town had tracks, Skiff Alley would have been on the wrong side of them. Home to Ash Beauty & Tattoo Parlor, Bookie McGee's (not a bookstore, but a betting establishment), and the Ratanas' Tasty Thai Hut, the backstreet wasn't even on the town's official map. And the alley wasn't wide enough for cars, much less a snowplow, so in winter it often iced over for months.

"Watch your step," Katrin said. Luckily, an overhang had protected a small strip of the alley during the storm, leaving a little walkway to the Ashes' salon and apartment over it.

They all clambered up the shadowy stairwell—even Rambo. Warped floorboards creaked under Jean's boots as she stepped inside, and her nose caught the lingering odor of burnt toast. Neither Katrin nor her mom was much of a cook.

Katrin tossed her wet coat onto the floor and kicked off her combat boots. "Leave your stuff anywhere," she said. "I'm not gonna tell you to clean up after yourself."

Katrin's dad had died just a few years after he and her

mom had moved to St. Polonius to open their salon together. Katrin had been very young. She'd shared this one-room apartment with her mom ever since.

Today it was quite a mess. More of Katrin's clothes were strewn across the floor, forming a dark and leathery path between the closet and the entrance. Dirty dishes covered the card table where the Ashes ate their meals. In the far corner of the studio was Katrin's "room," a curtained-off section with a mattress on the floor.

Micah, like Katrin, looked exhausted—Jean was the only one who had gotten any sleep the night before. He stared listlessly at a photo on the wall of a baby Katrin, squeezed in an embrace by her smiling father and purple-haired mother. "I miss our mom," he murmured to Jean. "And Dad. Are they really going to stay asleep until the spring?"

Not if I have anything to do with it, Jean thought. If some sort of illness had befallen the sleepers, a doctor from Bigsby could help. Though if it was a curse, and she had triggered it . . . She pushed that out of her mind as she helped Micah off with his coat.

Katrin held out a bag of Cap'n Lucky's Shrimp Crisps. "Hungry?"

Micah shook his head, even though he'd had no real lunch. Jean didn't like those crisps, but she shoved a handful into her mouth to set a good example for her brother. She swallowed quickly, forcing the dry, shrimpy mass down her throat.

"Thanks," she said to Katrin. "Micah, you sure you don't want some? They're, uh . . . good."

"Oh, all right." Micah took a couple of crisps. "Hey," he said, "who's gonna feed Mom and Dad while they're asleep? Don't they need to eat, too?"

A scientific question—finally, something Jean could answer. "The human body can last a long time without food," she told him. "That's why we have fat stores. Whether the sleepers will get dehydrated is the more important question. Luckily, it's not exactly hot out, so they should be fine for a few days. . . ."

Jean had meant for this explanation to comfort her brother, but Micah was looking more panicked by the second.

Katrin swooped in. "Hey, buddy," she said, slipping an arm around Micah's shoulders. "Old St. Polonius and his gang didn't eat or drink during their hibernation, and they woke up in the spring just fine, remember? So don't worry too much about your parents. The saints' miracle that put them to sleep will keep them healthy until it's time to wake up, okay?"

Micah nodded. "Okay."

Jean tried not to bristle. She'd always known that Katrin was a bigger believer in the saints than she was. Despite their wild hairdos and wardrobes, the Ashes attended First Polonian Church every Sunday, and the shelf over Katrin's mattress was crammed with saintly figurines. If what Katrin was telling Micah made him feel better, there was no real harm in it . . . but still, Jean was glad Mom wasn't there to see him so enthralled by what she'd call "codwash."

"Hey," Katrin continued, "I've got a bin of my old toys over in the corner. Wanna check it out?"

Micah's eyes brightened. "Do you have a farm set?" he asked. "Rambo kind of misses the other sheep."

Everyone glanced over at Rambo, who still hadn't made it off the tattered welcome mat. Jean wasn't sure how Micah interpreted this as the sheep pining for his fellows.

"Sure," Katrin said. "I've got plenty of toy animals. Well, mostly dragons and kraken, but I bet we can find a sheep or a goat or something in there. Come on."

Dark and early the next morning, Jean awoke to the faint sound of the snowplow rumbling one street over. Axel certainly was taking his new job seriously—Magnus would be pleased.

She pushed herself upright on Katrin's mattress. To her left, Micah slept with his mouth open, drool soaking into his pillowcase. Jean felt a twinge of guilt to see him soiling Katrin's bedding. Then again, Micah's saliva was probably more hygienic than, say, Rambo's bottom, which the sheep had plunked down on top of a different pillow on the kitchen floor.

Gross.

Katrin was asleep on the couch, snoring softly. As quietly as she could, Jean changed out of her borrowed pajamas and back into yesterday's clothes, braided her hair, and layered on her scarf, coat, and boots. If she snuck out now, she could make it down to the pier before the sun rose and anybody realized what she was up to. Maybe she'd even make it back from her trip before Katrin and Micah woke up.

She buttoned her coat, trying to still the nervous twitchiness in her fingers. Like most St. Polonian kids, she had been out on the water a few times, but she was no expert. She supposed she could wait a few hours and go to Magnus's office with her idea of sailing for Bigsby-on-the-Bay. She could ask Magnus to assign her a more experienced co-captain, or even a small crew.

But what if the town charter had a ban on seeking aid from rivals of St. Polonius? Magnus might not let her go at all.

If she went alone, though, she could truthfully claim ignorance about any rules. And if her plan worked, and she brought a doctor back from Bigsby who woke all the adults and teenagers, everyone would see that she had only been trying to help. She'd be a hero to her town, like St. Polonius himself had been—and more important, she'd be a hero to her family. She imagined her parents beaming as the newly woken mayor hung a shiny medal around *her* neck.

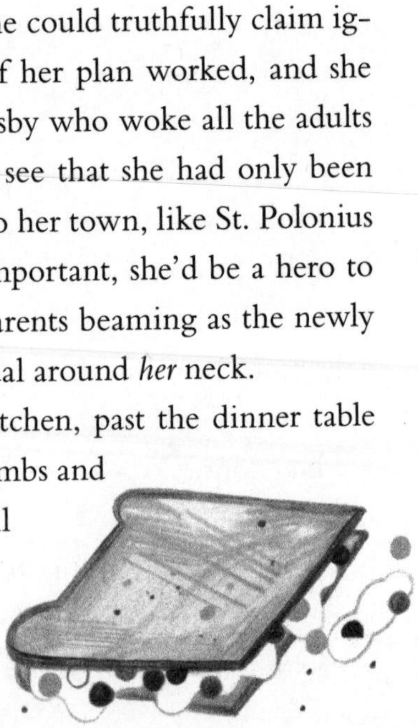

Jean tiptoed through the kitchen, past the dinner table still littered with last night's crumbs and crusts. Isara had been given until this morning to prepare the Tasty Thai Hut for its new role as town cafeteria, so Katrin raided the cupboards and made them all grilled gumdrop and cream cheese sandwiches. Jean had been hungry enough to choke down just one.

She'd considered telling her brother and Katrin about her Bigsby plan, but she knew that if she did, Micah would want to come with her, which seemed too dangerous. And if Katrin joined her, that would leave nobody to stay with Micah.

Plus, there was the chance that they would both try to stop her. After all, as far as she knew, no St. Polonian had set foot in Bigsby for years—not even Dr. Fields, who was from there.

The town of Bigsby-on-the-Bay was St. Polonius's chief rival—or had been a decade ago, when they were seaside towns of comparable size. But then the highway had come to Bigsby, and with it, tourists and money. Now Bigsby was a city, complete with cloud-scraping hotels, an iconic "Fjord-View Ferris Wheel," and—it was rumored—a brand-new Infinity Ice Rink on which people could literally skate off into the sunset. On clear nights, you could make out Bigsby's taunting neon glow from miles across the fjord.

"Bigsbyans' heads," Dr. Fields liked to say, "have gotten too big for their balaclavas."

Still, Jean knew that Dr. Fields had family over there; hanging in her lab were pictures of a brother and a sister. If Jean could contact one of them, she was sure they would help.

Her mittened hand was on the apartment doorknob when a soft *baaah* sounded behind her. Back in the kitchen,

Rambo had risen shakily to his feet and looked like he might follow Jean across the room.

"No, Rambo!" she hissed. "Go back to sleep!"

But he'd made up his mind, and the clopping of his hooves across the creaky floor sounded loud enough to wake all the hibernators. It was a miracle worthy of St. Polonius himself that everyone in the apartment was still asleep when the sheep reached the doorway.

"Okay, fine," she whispered to him. "You can come."

She opened the apartment door and shooed Rambo through it. This would actually make a perfect cover story for her mission. If anyone stopped her, she could tell them she was simply taking her sheep out to find some plants to eat.

But while the sheep had had no trouble following them all up the stairs yesterday, going down was another story. He spent more than a minute nervously toeing the edge of the landing, but try as Jean might with whispers and pats, she couldn't coax him to take the first step.

"Sorry, Rambo," she said finally, and using the padded leg of her snow boot, she gave his rump a shove. He let out a *baaah!* of surprise, but instinct must have taken over, because he clattered down the stairs without falling.

Outside, Rambo moseyed toward a fluffy snow pile to do his business, then looked around as if contemplating his next adventure. Before he could bolt, Jean unwound her scarf and tied it to his collar: a leash. She tugged him out of the alley.

It was three blocks to the harbor, and with the streets already plowed, they made a fast go of it. As they walked, Jean peered up at the mountains that hemmed their town in on three sides like a majestic backyard fence. The snow in St. Polonius had paused, but the puffy, cotton-wisp clouds that were already obscuring the mountain peaks told her that much more was on its way. This was probably her only window of opportunity to sail for Bigsby. She gave Rambo's leash a tug and started to jog.

At the pier, Jean could see a little ways onto the water. It was still too foggy to make out Bigsby's skyline, but conditions were decent. Her spirits rose like a boat cresting a wave.

But they crashed back down when she saw someone else climbing into the little red motorboat at the end of the pier—the very boat she'd planned to take out herself.

Keep close to the coast when yeh're fishin' to feed;
The sweet shallow waters provide all we need.
Don't float out too far once yeh've stepped up aboard;
Beware the fierce predators of the fjord!

–traditional St. Polonian fishing song

CHAPTER 9

"Hey!" Jean shouted. She ran down the pier, yanking Rambo behind her. Who had boarded the boat? She only saw the back of a head in a squarish fur-lined hat with earflaps. For a crazy second Jean thought it might be the boat's owner, Mr. Miller, awakened for a day at sea. But Mr. Miller had never been known to take his boat out before noon, and this sailor was too short and slight to be him anyway.

"Hey!" Jean cried again, and the mystery boatman turned around.

Isara Ratana.

"Oh!" they both said, and stepped back in surprise. Jean almost tripped over Rambo.

Isara's face, already pink from the cold, was turning red enough to match the boat. "Please don't tell the Smuthers twins—I mean, the police."

"Tell them what?"

"That I'm borrowing Mr. Miller's boat without permission," Isara said. "Though it's only to go fishing, I promise! I plan to bring it back right after."

"You're going fishing? All on your own?" Jean was impressed. Hauling in the large fish that swam in their northern waters often took the strength of two or three adults.

"I have to," Isara said. "The Tasty Thai Hut's pantry doesn't have enough food to feed the kids here for the whole winter. I was hoping to bring back some fish. But I see that I should have asked the mayor's permission first."

Jean laughed. "Well, I'm not going to tell B&B anything. Especially since I was heading down here hoping to, uh . . . borrow the boat myself."

Isara's eyes widened. "Were you going to fish, too?"

Jean hadn't even told Katrin about her plan—did she dare tell this boy, whom she hardly knew?

"Not exactly," she said. "But hey—why don't I go with you? It'll be safer with two of us." *Then,* she added in her head, *I can tell you where we're* really *heading once we're out on the water.* Even if Isara wasn't sympathetic to her cause, he might still zip her over to Bigsby if they were already half-way across the fjord.

"Three of us," Isara said with a smile.

"Huh?"

He nodded toward Jean's left, where Rambo was trying to chew through a mooring line.

"Rambo, quit that!" Jean managed to distract him from his fibrous snack. Down in the boat, Isara laughed.

"Sorry," she said, "but yeah—my brother wouldn't like me to leave his sheep on his own. So you get Rambo, too."

"No problem." Isara tossed two bright orange life vests up onto the pier.

By the time she had gotten a vest onto Rambo and coaxed him into the boat, the thick clouds overhead were glowing with sunlight around their edges. Jean glanced about warily, but the harbor was still desolate. Isara started the engine, grabbed hold of the tiller, and eased them out onto the water.

Most kids who had grown up in St. Polonius had basic boating skills, but Isara was an expert. He guided them through the choppy water with ease, even as Rambo bucked and baaed and generally made a wooly nuisance of himself.

"You've boated before!" Jean shouted over the noise of the engine.

"Yes, in Thailand! We lived by the sea." Water sprayed over the bow, and icy drops plinked against their faces. "A warmer sea than this one, though."

The morning fog rolled in around the boat, swallowing

up the pier behind them. The fjord's frigid waves whapped against the hull, and Jean huddled close to Rambo for warmth.

After about ten minutes, Isara cut the engine and pulled out a bag of fishing gear. Jean stood up unsteadily.

"So, Isara," she started, "bringing back fish to feed the kids would be great. Do you know what would be even better, though? Bringing back help from—"

But the rest of her sentence was drowned out by a much louder voice—one that seemed to come directly out of the mist ahead of them.

"Good morning, ladies and gentlemen, and welcome to your sunrise whale-watching cruise!"

"What was that?" Isara peered into the fog.

Jean clapped her mittens. "It's a tourist boat! From Bigsby!" Help was nearer than she'd hoped!

"A tourist boat? How *big* a tourist boat?"

"Probably pretty big . . . Why?"

"Because we haven't got radar!" Isara gasped. "And in this fog, we won't see the vessel until it's on top of us! It could flip us in a second." He yanked on the engine starter, then gave the tiller a hard pull to the right. "We have to turn back."

"What?" Jean lurched toward the rear of the boat. "Isara, wait! They could help us! They could help wake up our parents!"

But Isara's hand stayed firm. "Not if they drown us first!"

Before she even knew what she was doing, Jean had grabbed hold of the tiller herself. Using all her strength, she wrenched it back in the opposite direction.

Surprised, he let go. The boat swung wildly back to the left and Isara fell against the side, almost landing on Rambo, who squealed.

"I'm sorry!" Jean shouted, still pulling as hard as she could, "but we have to get to those whale watchers!"

Isara scrambled to his feet. "It's too dangerous!" he yelled. "As captain, I order you to stop!"

"Captain? You stole this boat!"

"Yes, but I stole it before you did!" Isara lunged for the tiller. "Which means that *I'm* the captain—and this is a mutiny!"

The motorboat zigged and zagged as Jean and Isara struggled for control, and the booming voice sounded again. *"Ladies and gentlemen, please get your binoculars ready! The captain has spotted a disturbance in the water off the starboard side!"*

The outline of the enormous tourist ship popped through the fog—so close, and moving toward their little boat so fast, that Jean, Isara, and Rambo could do nothing but scream.

Your Bigsbyan holiday
won't be complete without

A WHALE-WATCHING CRUISE

ON SCORPION CRUISE LINES!

OBSERVE
whales, sharks, dolphins, Kraken
and other creatures of the sea
in their natural habitats!

Cruise in luxury in the beautiful northern sunshine![1]
Unlimited drinks included![2]
By popular demand,
season now extends into October![3]

BOOK NOW!!!

[1]Sunshine not guaranteed. [2]Unlimited water is included.
Sunrise cruises include one complimentary mimosa.
[3]This one is true.

CHAPTER 10

Isara had been right. A whale-watching cruiser was about to plow straight into their boat, tossing them to their icy, watery deaths—*if* its huge rotors didn't tear them to bloody pieces first.

Jean and Isara threw themselves against the tiller, and this time they were pushing in the same direction. The motor-boat's course curved to the right, but not enough. The tourist ship bore down, so close that they could read the name on its hull: *Scorpion of the Seas.*

Isara grunted something. Jean sent up a fresh prayer, begging the saints for a maritime miracle. Rambo baaed.

And then—

"Ahoy!" cried a voice from the Bigsbyan ship. "I see something! Stop!"

The *Scorpion*'s engine cut out, and the ship slowed *just* enough for the motorboat to squeak past its bow with inches to spare.

A wave of sweet relief washed over Jean—followed immediately by a wave of frigid seawater, which knocked all three of them to the boat's floor.

"It's a whale!"

"No, it's a dolphin!"

"Naw, see—it's red! It must be a giant arctic crab!"

Sweet St. Polonius, Jean thought. *Have none of these people ever seen an actual sea creature before?*

Groping for the side of the boat with a very wet mitten, Jean hauled herself to her feet.

"Good gracious!" another tourist voice cried. "It's a human!"

"Two humans!" a different voice shouted as Isara pulled himself upright.

The motorboat's engine had died, leaving them bobbing in the current alongside the ship. An eager line of faces gazed down over the *Scorpion*'s railing at them. None of the tourists were dressed for the weather—several wore baseball caps, and one sported a Stetson. A few held tropical-looking drinks. Still, they were adults—and awake.

"Help!" Jean shrieked, waving frantically up at the tourists. "Hello, we need your—"

But the booming voice cut her off. *"Ladies and gentlemen, we have a special treat for you today—a rare sighting of some of the fjord's most elusive creatures!"*

Huh? Jean glanced over at a very wet Isara, who looked just as confused as she was.

"If you look starboard," the voice continued, *"you'll have a very fine view of two natives from the isolated settlement of St. Polonius-on-the-Fjord!"*

"Oooooh!" Flashes burst through the mist as the tourists snapped pictures. Jean waved her hands more wildly.

"As you have probably read in your guidebooks, St. Polonius is notorious for its bizarre cultural practices. In fact, it appears that one of the natives is currently performing a dance, perhaps trying to summon up her ancient saint of the sea."

Jean froze, hands above her head.

"Alas, the dance seems to have reached its conclusion. But you can still view the traditional dress of this rarely observed culture!"

The cameras flashed again, and Jean looked down at her wet, bedraggled self.

"Note the bright orange vests," the announcer continued, *"cut in the old-fashioned St. Polonian style. In this society, orange is considered the color of luck."*

The announcer was just making things up! Couldn't the

tourists see that? "These are life vests!" Jean yelled. "And our parents are sick—please help!"

"Hark!" the announcer cried. *"The female native is trying to communicate! However, she speaks with the Old Polonish accent, which is impossible for outsiders to understand."*

"This is better than whales!" the Stetson-wearing man exclaimed.

A hand rested gently upon Jean's shoulder. "Let's go," Isara said. "These people are not going to help us."

"No!" Jean shrugged him off. Hot tears sprang into her eyes, making them the only parts of her body that weren't shaking with cold. "We *have* to make them understand! Please, Isara!"

The wind seemed to quiet just long enough for Jean to hear Isara sigh. "I've had experience with tourists, Jean," he said. "Thailand is full of them. Most aren't bad people, but . . . they don't like to involve themselves in local problems."

"But they're *adults*! How can they—"

"Look!" another tourist yelled. "There's an animal in the boat with those natives! Dressed up in their lucky color!"

Jean felt a nudge at her leg; Rambo had finally crawled out from under the wooden seat.

"Ladies and gentlemen . . ." The announcer's voice dropped to an amplified whisper. *"We may have the good fortune to witness a very rare ritual! It appears that the natives have brought a sacrificial ram out in their boat as a gift to their saint of the sea! If we all watch quietly, we may get to see them throw it in."*

"Ooooh!" the tourists cried.

"WHAT?" Jean dropped to her knees and threw her arms around Rambo. "Don't listen to them, boy!"

"Toss it!" a tourist cried.

"Yeah," called another, "throw it in!"

Jean released Rambo and straightened back up as a collective moan of disappointment sounded from the *Scorpion*'s deck.

"Maybe they need help!" someone yelled.

For a split second, Jean's heart jumped. *Yes, help!*

"Hey, Cap'n!" the Stetson man called. "Fire up them engines and give this boat a little push!"

"Yes!" cried the others. "Push, push!"

The engine of the *Scorpion* growled to life, and the tourists cheered. Slowly, the ship turned in the water, its bow aiming once again for Jean and Isara's motorboat.

"Jean!" Isara shouted into her ear. "Go, NOW!"

She knew he was right. These tourists would capsize their boat to get a better show.

Jumping over Rambo, Jean grabbed hold of the tiller as Isara pulled on the soaked engine's starter string. The motor sputtered and caught. Leaning hard on the tiller, Jean swung their boat toward home.

As they moved off, she looked back for a final glimpse of the bulky *Scorpion,* still trying to turn itself, before it was swallowed up by the fog.

She was so mad she stepped to the edge of the motorboat and spit straight into the fjord-water. The sea spit back with spray. Jean cursed, and Rambo baaed as freezing water pooled around his hooves on the boat floor. Isara was silent; he'd taken over the tiller.

Jean thought about begging Isara to turn again and take them to Bigsby. But the fog was thickening by the second and starting to drop bits of snow. The blizzard was returning, and this time would probably ice in St. Polonius's small harbor. Jean's one chance was gone.

The steeple of First Polonian Church came into view through the mist. A minute later, they could make out the pier . . . and the two figures standing upon it.

Tall, broad, and dressed alike—right down to their shiny police badges. The Smuthers twins were waiting for them.

CHAPTER 11

"Citizens, good morning!" Bartleby leered over the edge of the pier as Isara and Jean docked. "Or should we say 'Ahoy!'?"

Isara looked grim, and Jean remembered how worried he'd been about getting caught "borrowing" Mr. Miller's boat. "Don't worry," she whispered. "I'll handle this."

Bertha's nasal voice pierced the air. "What takes you two out on the fjord on such a"—she gazed around at the freezing fog—"fine day?"

Jean held her wet head high and tried to control her chattering teeth. "We were out f-fishing," she announced. "You know—so the kids in this town can get f-fed."

"You went fishing," Bartleby said, "and came back with . . . one sheep?"

Rambo baaed, as if on cue.

"Hush!" Jean hissed at him. She didn't want B&B to get any ideas about feeding Rambo to the hungry masses. "This ram happens to have an excellent nose for cod." Sheep are vegetarians—but maybe the Smuthers twins didn't know that. "We took him out to help us, but there were no bites today."

"Not a single bite?" Bertha asked. She had removed her nightstick from her utility belt and was smacking it rhythmically into her gloved palm. Every time it hit, Isara winced. Had he been robbed or bullied by the twins in the past? Jean wouldn't put it past them to gang up on the "new kid."

"What a shame," Bertha continued. "Well, Chef Ratana, I guess you'll have to manage with the supplies you have. The mayor went by the Tasty Thai Hut this morning to inspect your breakfast preparations, but when he found you missing, he called us in to investigate."

Jean groaned inwardly. Of course Magnus was already checking that people were following the rules.

"Sorry," Isara mumbled. "I'll start the breakfast right away." He gathered his fishing gear and scrambled up the ladder to the pier, not even sparing a glance for Jean. She didn't blame him; her mission had failed, and she'd wrecked his fishing efforts.

"I'll escort you back to your place of business," Bertha told him, and Isara could only nod miserably. "And my brother," she continued to Jean, "will take care of *you.*"

Take care of her?

"Come on." Bartleby stepped down onto the ladder. "Let's get your *fishing sheep* out of that boat."

Even working together, they were barely able to hoist a fidgety Rambo up onto the pier.

"The mayor asked to see you," Bartleby said.

"He did?" Jean gulped. "What does he want?"

"That's his business. Let's go." He took her arm.

Trapped in Bartleby's grip, Jean shuffled toward town. Thick snowflakes were falling, and soon she didn't even care where she was going, as long as it was indoors and dry. Maybe Magnus had a fireplace.

The mayor's office was located on the second floor of town hall, and Rambo balked at the steep marble staircase. Grudgingly, Bartleby said he'd stay downstairs with the sheep.

On the office door, the plaque that said OFFICE OF MAYOR THEOBALD H. KING was crossed out. MAGNUS! had been spelled out in crayon on it instead.

"Do you like the sign?" Liddy Dowell asked. The six-year-old daughter of the mayor's assistant sat behind a desk by the office door, her short legs dangling from her mother's swivel chair. "I made it!"

"Very nice," Jean said, and Liddy beamed.

"The mayor will see you now!" she cried, and pressed a button on her desk. A buzzer sounded, and Jean heard the lock on the mayor's door disengage with a click. She stepped inside.

The office was vast and mostly empty, save a large desk and an oval rug with the town's symbol, a reproduction of Captain Polonius's three-masted ship, the *Jolly Narwhal.* There was a fireplace (unlit, alas!) and a bookcase full of thick volumes, several labeled *Laws.*

Magnus sat with his feet up on the desk, staring at an oil portrait of his father on the far wall. Jean supposed that even Magnus the Magnificent missed his parents.

He leapt to his feet when he noticed her. "Jean Huddy! Exactly the person I've been hoping to see this morning. Come in, come in. Sit."

Wary of soiling the fancy rug with her wet boots, Jean skirted it and sat. On Magnus's desk was a jar full of round pink bonbons dusted in sugar: thistleberry candies. Wonderfully sweet and tart, they had been made at home by St. Polonians for centuries; the mayor's proposed plant would start churning them out to be sold all around the country. Jean's stomach rumbled.

"Please, help yourself," Magnus said.

"Thanks." Jean fished a fat candy out and popped it in her mouth. It fizzed on her tongue, releasing a gush of sour juice.

"You're probably wondering why I sent for you, Jean." Magnus leaned forward. "As you may remember, our conversation at the festival was interrupted. There was something important I wanted to ask you."

Oh, no. Founders' Day. Was he about to ask her . . . ?

"Magnush—"

The candy was taking up her entire mouth. As she cast around for something to spit it into, Magnus kept talking. "Great saints, this is a bit embarrassing to discuss. But . . . what I wanted to know is . . ." He cleared his throat. "Did you really eat your Sacred Bear Liver on Founders' Day?"

"What?" A mist of pink juice flew out of Jean's lips, dotting the papers on the desk. Magnus pulled a box of tissues out of a desk drawer and used one to blot them dry; Jean, sure she had turned as pink as her candy, grabbed a tissue and finally spit it out.

"Magnus—"

"That's Mayor King, if you please."

Seriously? "Okay, sure. Mayor King, I . . ."

But how to answer? Jean's parents hadn't wanted her to tell *anyone* what had happened.

She had to turn the tables. "Why are you asking me this? You were there in the tent; you saw me eat it. Is this how your mayorship is going to be—hauling kids in and interrogating them whenever you want for no good reason?"

"Of course not," he huffed. "But I'm charged with maintaining law and order. And a citizen of age not eating their liver . . . you know as well as I do that that's a serious crime. If not properly punished by me, who knows what kind of retribution it might trigger from the saints? Or might have already triggered?" One eyebrow rose.

Magnus thought Jean had caused the hibernation.

Had she?

Without a doctor from Bigsby to examine the sleepers, it

was impossible to know for sure. But Jean didn't think that the saints—if they really existed—would punish two hundred and fifty people for one girl's mistake. And the original hibernation had *saved* people's lives; it was a blessing, not a curse.

Mom wouldn't sit there and let the old mayor accuse her of things; Jean shouldn't take it from Magnus. She stood up and stared straight at him. "You have no proof that I did anything wrong."

"True." Magnus stood, then glanced at his now-speckled papers. "But if any were to turn up . . . say, evidence . . . or a witness . . . Well, I don't get to choose which laws I enforce any more than I get to choose how a word is spelled. There's only one right way, and I have to do my job."

"Right," Jean said. "Your *job*."

But Magnus didn't seem to catch her sarcasm. "Speaking

of jobs, you're supposed to be out at the sheep farm during your mother's hibernation."

Well, if Magnus wanted to discuss *her* job, Jean would take advantage of the opportunity. "Mayor King, I don't think that sheep farming is the best way for me to contribute my skills to St. Polonius-on-the-Fjord while we're in this crisis."

"But Jean," he said with a frown, "the town charter tells us that taking over our parents' jobs is exactly what we must do in this situation. I thought I explained that yesterday."

Why did Magnus have to do everything so by-the-book? "You did," she said. "The thing is, the farm doesn't need me. My mom set up an amazing automated system that can keep the sheep fed and watered for weeks. And besides, if my brother is supposed to work at our dad's university office here in town, I'd rather not be so far away from him. He's only eight."

"You want to stay close to your brother, do you?" Magnus asked.

She nodded. Her idea of getting to Bigsby was dead for now. Watching out for Micah all winter wouldn't earn her any medals, but it was what her parents would have wanted—and what she wanted, too. She took a deep breath. "If it's possible, I'd like to have a different work assignment."

Magnus blinked. "A what?"

"A reassignment," Jean said. "Yesterday, you made exceptions to the town charter's rule for younger kids and for kids of single parents. Doesn't it make sense to make one more exception, for people whose parents' jobs are already done, or aren't essential?"

Magnus's eyebrows scrunched together. "I *had* been thinking about implementing such a system," he said, "perhaps a few weeks down the road."

"Well, why not start it today, with me?" Jean asked. "I already know the perfect job. Dr. Mary Fields, the biochemist, doesn't have any kids, but she does lots of interesting experiments. I already help her out with them sometimes. And besides, her office is right next to my dad's, so working there would let me keep an eye on Micah. If I could take over doing *her* job, it would be good for everyone."

"Dr. Fields?" Magnus asked. "The *Bigsbyan* scientist we were talking about at the festival?"

From the way Magnus said "Bigsbyan," you'd have thought Dr. Fields was an enemy soldier. Jean had no great love of Bigsby after the tourist boat encounter that morning, but still, this seemed unfair.

"*You're* the one who pointed out that Bigsby is right across the fjord," she said. "It's not like it's another country—though even if it were, that wouldn't make Dr. Fields and her work any less important to our town."

Magnus stroked his medal, then looked up. "You make a strong case, Jean. But what if someone else wants that job? It wouldn't be fair for me to give it to you simply because you asked first."

Jean hadn't thought of this. "I guess not. . . ."

"But if I were to test you—you know, on your aptitude to take on Dr. Fields's work—that would show whether you were capable, wouldn't it?"

"Um, sure." Science, though, was the one subject where

Jean did better than Magnus at school. What qualified him to test her? "If you want to go down to Dr. Fields's office, I can show you the last experiment I helped her—"

"That won't be necessary. I can give you a test right now, if you're ready." He went to the bookcase in the corner and grabbed the dictionary.

"Please spell *heterogeneous.*"

Jean felt like she'd been slapped with icy fjord-water all over again. "You want me to take a spelling test?"

"Not just any spelling test." Magnus sat behind the desk. "A test for science words, since you'd like to work as a biochemist."

Jean closed her eyes. She had to be the worst speller in St. Polonius—and Magnus knew it.

"Look," he said, "I won't insist that you get one hundred percent of the words correct. But how about two out of three?"

His medal sparkled at his chest. *He isn't trying to be horrible,* Jean told herself. *He just thinks spelling is the best kind of exam.* After all, it had worked out well for him. Her luck had been terrible so far today, but maybe it was about to change.

"All right," she said, "I'll do my best." She sat.

"Good. Then, *heterogeneous.* Would you like to know the origin of the word? You're allowed to ask."

Jean doubted that information would help her. "No thanks. Um, *heterogeneous. H . . . E . . . T . . . O*—"

Thunk! Magnus's fist rapped against the desk. "I'm afraid that's incorrect. *Heterogeneous* is spelled *H-E-T-E-R-O-G-E-N-E-O-U-S.*"

"Right," Jean said weakly.

Magnus seemed energized now. He flipped through the dictionary again as Jean prayed to those slippery saints for an easier word.

"Ah, this is a good one for biochemistry," he said. *"Deoxyribonucleic."*

Jean sat up straighter. "You know," she said, "a real scientist would never bother writing that word out in her notes. She would abbreviate it *D-N,* as part of DNA."

Magnus looked up from the book. "Hmm. I suppose that's a clever answer."

Jean beamed. She was one word away now from taking over Dr. Fields's job. Scowling slightly, Magnus flipped through the book again—then closed it. *"Salt."*

Salt? Jean thought back to the day after school when she had helped Dr. Fields mix up a salty preserving solution. She pictured the label on the jar of white crystals. *"S-A-L-T."*

"Very good," said Magnus. "Now, how about *fry*?"

"Didn't you say two out of three?" Jean asked. And what did the word *fry* have to do with biology or chemistry, anyway? She supposed that the offspring of a fish was called a fry . . .

"Are you saying that you can't spell a short little word like *fry*?" Magnus asked.

"Of course I can: *F-R-Y.* But—"

"And one more," Magnus continued. *"Mix."*

Well, that one was easy enough, too. *"M-I-X,"* Jean spelled. Perhaps that very morning, she'd be mixing tinctures in Dr. Fields's lab.

"Correct," Magnus said, "and congratulations. You've proven yourself qualified to begin your new job assignment as assistant cook at the Tasty Thai Hut."

"*What?*" Jean blinked. "I was applying to be a biochemist."

"Yes," Magnus said, "but you failed that test within the first two words. So I administered a different one."

"But those were all science words!"

"No, they were cooking words. And you did a very good job with them."

He'd tricked her.

"You asked not to be sent back to work on your farm," he continued, "and yesterday, Isara requested help for his kitchen. So now you have a new, more useful job, right here in town. That's what you wanted, isn't it?" He rearranged some papers on his desk.

Jean's boots stomped the floor as she stood. "This isn't fair."

Magnus looked up; he seemed surprised that she was still there. "Well, I'm sorry that you feel that way, but as mayor I need to make all sorts of difficult decisions. This is what I feel is best for the town. I'm sure that if you think about it, you'll agree."

Jean's mouth opened and closed. She'd gone head to head with Magnus the Magnificent—and, as usual, he had won.

She stormed out, making sure to leave a wet bootprint smack in the middle of the *Jolly Narwhal.*

CHAPTER 12

The town hall's vast lobby was deserted, with Bartleby and Rambo nowhere to be seen.

Great. Jean should never have trusted Bartleby to watch Micah's sheep. A narrow hallway branched off from the lobby to her right; maybe they'd gone that way.

The hallway had three doors: two that led to the men's and ladies' toilets, and one that had no sign. Jean tried the knob for the unmarked door, and it turned. Inside, the room was dark.

"Rambo?" she called. She groped along the wall for a light switch, flicked it on, and caught her breath.

Bodies carpeted the room.

Sleeping adults and teenagers lay in rows, with only the narrowest aisles between them. There lay the school headmaster, Mr. Johanssen, his thick beard resting on his padded vest. His wife, the local librarian, sprawled next to him, her knitted hat forming a pillow for her blond head. Jean imagined their daughter, Eliza, arranging them, making sure they were comfortable.

A few aisles over, Jean spotted Ms. Mitchell—Micah's teacher—and her partner, Ms. Seidel, who ran the general store. Both were covered with tweedy wool coats; their daughter, Jillian, must have done that. And next to the podium at the far end of the room lay Mayor King himself, between Magnus's elegantly dressed mother and Burt Miller, the old restaurant owner. Mr. Miller had no children, but Magnus must have tended to him, too, because he was tucked in under a long black cloak and looked as content in his slumber as the Kings did.

At the far end of the last row of sleepers, Jean spotted someone who had not been tended to. Limbs akimbo and long gray hair disheveled, Dr. Mary Fields looked like she'd been dumped in a heap and left there.

Jean hurried over. She dropped to one knee and rolled Dr. Fields gently onto her side so she could tug out the old coat pinned beneath her. Unlike nearby sleepers, Dr. Fields had a wrinkled brow, and her lips moved every few seconds, as if she was on the verge of talking. But she didn't make a sound.

As the coat came free, it fell open to reveal something white sticking out of an inner pocket. Jean pulled out a piece of paper, half crumpled, as if it had been stuck inside in haste.

"Jean Huddy!"

Jean shoved the paper into her own pocket and quickly covered Dr. Fields with the coat. Bertha, Bartleby, and—thank goodness!—Rambo stood in the doorway.

"What are you doing in here?" Bartleby demanded.

"I was . . . looking for the bathroom," Jean said.

Bertha glanced over her shoulder at the door clearly marked Ladies. "We know she can't spell," she told her brother. "I guess she can't read, either."

Jean's fist clenched in her pocket. *Don't start a fight with B&B.*

"Your stupid sheep had to go to the bathroom, too," said Bartleby, "so I took him outside. It was disgusting."

Good, Jean thought. Stuffing the paper farther down into her coat pocket, she stood up and picked her way through the sleepers toward the door. "I'll take him, then. I'll use the bathroom at the Tasty Thai Hut—I've been assigned to work there."

"We know," Bertha said. "The mayor briefed me. We'll escort you over."

As the twins marched beside Jean, the snowy streets of St. Polonius seemed to come alive. The front doors of little houses opened and shut, and children streamed out, older ones pulling younger ones by the hand or carrying them. Without adults around to dress them, many hadn't bothered with winter hats or scarves, and as far as Jean could tell, no one had brushed their hair, either. Everyone was heading toward Skiff Alley and the Tasty Thai Hut for breakfast.

Jean had never been to the restaurant; unless they took a summertime picnic to the fjord-front, her family rarely ate away from home. In fact, most of the adults in town claimed not to have tried it. They would say they preferred traditional St. Polonian food—like the sturgeon-and-reindeer pies Mr. Miller served at Ye Olde Mill Inn—to anything new or foreign.

But Katrin, who had a good view of the Tasty Thai Hut from her apartment, said they were all liars. They might not admit to it, but she saw a steady stream of customers visiting the restaurant's tiny takeout window each night, slinking into the darkness with paper bags full of hot curry and noodles.

Bertha and Bartleby delivered Jean to the takeout window, and Bartleby banged on the shutter. "Ratana! Open up, in the name of the law!"

B&B were taking their jobs *way* too seriously.

The kitchen door beside the window opened; Isara stood there, an apron thrown over his clothes and a yellow bandana holding his hair off his shining brow. Steam poured out of the kitchen and into the alleyway.

"What is it?" he snapped. "I'm extremely busy."

"Attitude, Ratana," Bertha said. "Be nicer to us, or we won't bring you any more helpers." She gave the back of Jean's leg a little nudge with her boot.

Jean stumbled forward. "Hi again."

"Oh, no," Isara groaned. "Not you."

Bertha snickered. "This should work out well."

Jean glowered at her, then turned to Isara. "Yup, it's me!" she said in her cheeriest voice. "At your service, ready to work!"

Isara looked her over. "Do you have any kitchen experience?"

Jean thought. She knew how to set a table, and how to heat up leftovers. "Oh, yes. Years of it."

He sighed. "All right, then, come in. I have loads of hungry kids squeezed into the dining room, and breakfast is still a long way from ready."

"Have you seen my brother in there?" she asked quickly. "Because he might be worried about me. Also, someone's got to take care of Rambo."

"We'll find him and give him the sheep," Bartleby grunted. "And we want breakfast, too."

"And coffee!" Bertha piped up. "Our mother never starts her workday without a big cup of coffee. Lots of milk, and three sugars."

"Four sugars in mine," Bartleby said, and they marched around the corner to the restaurant's main entrance with Rambo.

"I don't have time to make special drinks," Isara muttered. "Now get in here."

The kitchen felt like a tiny, crowded sauna. To Jean's left was a set of burners; two enormous pots of boiling liquid shot steam into the air. To her right, a vast griddle glimmered with hot grease. She shrugged off her coat.

"Watch it!" Isara cried as a coat arm swept close to a lit burner. He snatched the coat, disappeared around a corner with it, and returned with work clothes.

"Put these on—they're my mother's. She's small, so they should fit. You can change in there." He gestured toward a half-open door.

"Thanks." Jean wished he were handing her a scientist's lab coat, but she took the bundle as Isara bent over a pot, whisking furiously.

Jean stepped into a pantry filled with bags, boxes, and cans. One corner was piled with sacks of jasmine rice; packages of noodles in various shapes and sizes filled a barrel. Shelves on the rear wall held cans with coconuts on the labels.

Finally, she was alone and could look at Dr. Fields's paper. She groped for her pocket—but it was in her *coat* pocket, which Isara had taken away.

"Jean, are you ready?" Isara called. "I could use help out here!"

"Hold your sea horses," she muttered, and pulled off her clothes. Compared to her stiff and salty snow pants, Isara's mother's checkered cooking slacks felt like silk.

She pulled on a blue T-shirt that said TASTY THAI HUT

and a bandana like Isara's to hold back her stiff braids. Boots on again, she returned to the kitchen. This might not have been the job she wanted, but she owed the town her best effort. Even if she couldn't help the hibernators, her parents might be proud of her if she did a good job cooking for the kids of St. Polonius.

Isara barely looked up from frying omelets. "Start with the tea," he said. "You know how to make tea, right?"

"Of course," Jean lied.

"Good. Tea leaves are on that shelf, canned milk is in the pantry. Make it half strength, though—we don't have enough tea to last the winter, and the kids shouldn't have that much caffeine anyway."

How hard could it be? Jean knew hot water was involved, so she pulled a pot out from the shelf under the sink and turned on the tap to fill it. It was starting to bubble on top of a lit burner when Isara turned around from the griddle. A yelp escaped his lips.

"What are you doing?"

"Boiling water for tea?"

"You don't use that pot. That pot is for squid."

"Squid," Jean said. "Right."

"You use the *kettle* for tea." Isara pointed to the enormous kettle that sat on a cart right next to the burners. "Are you sure you've made tea before?"

"Sure," Jean said. "Kettle, got it."

He turned back to the griddle and Jean, cheeks flaming, turned off the burner and dumped the potful of water down the sink drain. It *did* smell a little squiddy—ugh.

The kettle, on the other hand, didn't smell like fish, but as Jean was filling it, she realized that it didn't smell like tea, either. Shouldn't it? Or did you mix the boiled water with the tea leaves in another vessel?

She looked over her shoulder to ask, but Isara was hustling out to the dining room with a loaded tray. The griddle was bare now; he'd already made a meal for a hundred kids, and she hadn't yet produced a single cup of tea.

She turned the water up to full blast to fill the kettle faster, lugged it to the stove, and twisted the burner button as high as it would go. Then she headed to the pantry for cans of milk.

On the shelves sat cans of pineapple, water chestnuts, and a spiny fruit called rambutan. There were also many cans with coconuts on them. The word *milk* caught her eye underneath a picture of a coconut.

Top-grade, extra-thick, preservative-free coconut milk, the can said. *Imported from Thailand.*

Isara had told her to use canned milk. This must be it.

The can said: *eight servings.* Jean grabbed several and put them on a kitchen counter. She took a can opener and began to cut them open.

She was on her third one when Isara returned. "What—what are you doing?"

"I'm opening the milk," Jean said. "You know, for the tea."

"Nononono!" Isara was close to despair. "This is coconut milk, for curries. It's hard to come by in this part of the world. Expensive! How many have you opened already? Three? Oh, my parents would kill me if they were awake."

"I'm—I'm sorry!" Jean cried. "You said canned milk, and this was the only thing I saw in the pantry that said *milk,* so . . ." For the second time that morning, hot tears started to pool in her eyes. Couldn't she do *anything* right?

Isara's voice softened. "Just leave the coconut milk. I'll use it in the lunch, it's not a problem. I should have shown you what to do." Gently, he took Jean by the arm and led her to a box in the pantry labeled *MILK.*

He pulled out several small cans of sweetened condensed milk. "These are for tea. I'll teach you how to make it."

Back in the kitchen, he found a large insulated pitcher and showed Jean how to measure tea leaves into the bottom. He then filled the pitcher with hot water from the kettle and, after three minutes, filtered the leaves out by pouring the tea through a strainer into another pitcher.

"Next," he said, "we add the condensed milk. It's already sweet, see, so we don't need sugar." He passed an open can to Jean and encouraged her to sample a bit. It was like a creamier version of thistleberry honey—yum.

They scraped the condensed milk into the huge pitcher; then Jean stirred the tea with a long wooden spoon. Finally, Isara poured Jean a cup so she could try it and know how it was supposed to taste. Her first sip was milky and sweet—very different from the tart thistleberry tea she knew, but no less delicious. It warmed her insides right down to her toes.

"Why are you suddenly being nice to me?" Jean blurted. "I ruined your fishing trip, and I almost ruined breakfast."

Isara took his time rinsing out a sticky milk can. Finally, he said, "I know what it's like to . . . be in a place where nothing makes sense. Where you have to pretend you know the rules, even when you don't. Sometimes, you need someone to show you the way."

She knew he wasn't only talking about tea-making. But who had shown him and his family the way when they had first arrived in St. Polonius-on-the-Fjord? Jean hadn't done it—and neither had anyone else.

Maybe she could make up for that a little. "Welcome," she said, a year late.

Isara's brow furrowed. "I think you mean 'thank you'?"

She laughed. "Of course. Thank you." She turned back to the pitcher of tea. "Now what?"

"Now," Isara said, "serve the tea. And good luck." For the first time since she'd arrived in the kitchen, a hint of a smile crossed his face. "It's a madhouse out there."

Jean stood tall, screwed the top onto the pitcher, heaved it off the counter, and pushed through the swinging door.

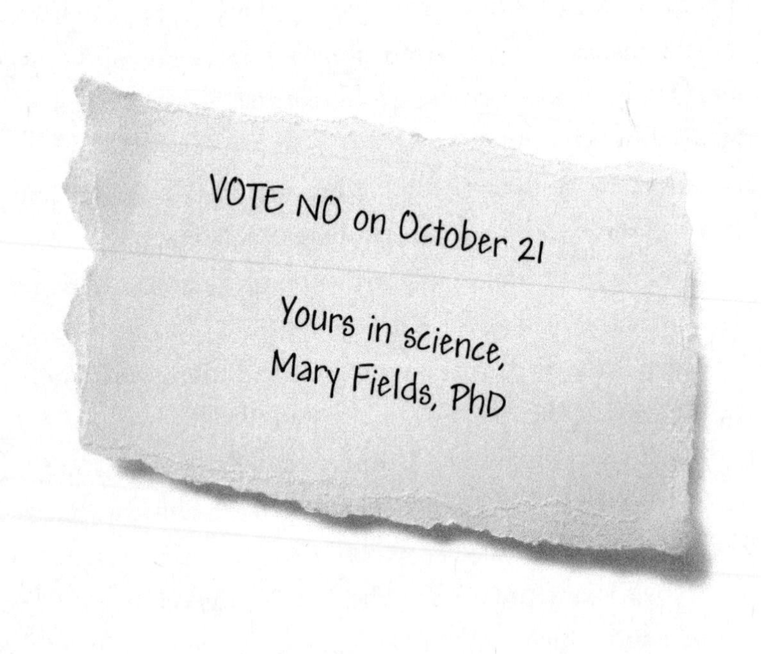

CHAPTER 13

Madhouse was an understatement. Kids were shrieking, shouting, and zooming all over the very small dining room.

A saucer skidded across the floor at Jean's feet; Joey Peterson had whacked it with a hockey stick.

Alaria Daly zoomed by on a skateboard, the fairy wings of a Halloween costume flapping on her back.

A boy with long hair was literally hanging from the rafters.

"Axel Gorson, you get down from there this minute!" Jean shouted.

She took a step in his direction and her feet almost flew out from under her. The floor was slick with tracked-in snow and ice, and a large pile of snow had built up right inside the restaurant's main door. Could that much have blown in from the blizzard?

Six-year-olds Annemarie Hammerstein and Lars Ludavisk were heading for the snow pile with buckets—at least someone was doing something useful! But then Jean did a double take. The kids weren't using the buckets to remove the snow. They were adding *more* to the pile.

"Hey!" she called. "What do you think you're doing?"

Lars shot Jean a chocolate-stained grin. "We're gonna build an indoor snowman!"

"And *then* we're gonna give him a brain transplant!" Annemarie cried. "I brought my mom's scalpel! Look!" Jean shrank back as Annemarie brandished a sharp-edged metal stick.

Where on earth was Magnus? Maintaining order was his job! Jean finally spotted him huddled at a corner table with B&B and a few other kids: his new assistant, Liddy Dowell; Kris Thornhill, whose dad was pastor of First Polonian Church; and Amelia Willoughby, whose mom ran the town's day-care center.

Jean sidled up and listened in on their conversation.

"Interim Day Care Matron Willoughby," Magnus said to Amelia, "have you confirmed that the day-care center has enough construction paper and markers for the project?"

"Yes, Mr. Mayor."

"Excellent. Please make sure that the children use permanent markers *only* when making their posters for town use. Interim Pastor Thornhill, how is your holiday sermon coming?"

"Not bad, thank you, Mr. Mayor," Kris said. "If you'd like to take a look . . ."

"I'd be happy to review it for you," Magnus said. "Please talk to my secretary to make an appointment at my office. Now, Interim Constables—"

"Hey, there's the waitress with the coffee!" Bartleby cried. "Waitress, over here!"

It took Jean a second to realize that he was calling her. She stepped forward, trying to look like she hadn't been eavesdropping.

"Jean Huddy!" Magnus said heartily. "How is your first morning at the new job?"

The job you forced on me, Jean thought. It took all her self-control to keep from pouring hot tea right into his lap.

She couldn't keep the sarcasm out of her voice, though. "Oh, it's going swimmingly, thanks. All our customers are behaving *so* maturely!" Just then, an airplane made of a folded napkin plummeted, nose-first, into Magnus's bowl of rice porridge.

His blue eyes snapped open, and he seemed to see the room for the first time. "Great saints—this is completely unacceptable!"

Finally, we agree on something, Jean thought. Magnus would stand up, make a speech, and get everyone to settle down.

But he leaned back. "Constables?"

"We're on it," Bertha said. She rose and whipped her nightstick out from her belt; Bartleby followed.

A dark-haired little boy, maybe four years old, careened across Bertha's path. "You!" Bertha hollered, catching him by the sleeve of his T-shirt. "What are you doing out of your seat? SIDDOWN! Hold him, brother."

The room fell silent as Bartleby grabbed the boy's shoulders. Bertha raised her nightstick.

"No!" Jean lunged forward, but Magnus had already sprung from his seat and grasped Bertha's arm.

"No need for violence! That is"—Magnus's voice grew louder—"as long as *everyone follows the rules*."

The little boy started to sob. "I was just—coming over—to ask the waitress—for a drink! I'm th-th-thirsty!"

"I don't care if your mouth is as dry as a dehydrated octopus," Bertha snarled. "You'll sit with your family members and eat the breakfast you've been given. This is your final warning."

"And that goes for all of you!" Bartleby boomed.

Jean glimpsed Katrin and Micah at a table in the far corner. Her brother's eyes were wide. All over the dining room, kids slunk back to their seats. There weren't nearly enough tables and chairs for everyone, so most of them squatted on the slushy floor, balancing plates in their laps.

Magnus nodded and sat. Something bugged Jean, though. Magnus had stopped B&B from hurting the boy . . . just like he had called them off yesterday when they'd threatened Isara, and then herself. He was always right there to intervene; it was almost too convenient.

Could these scenes be staged?

Most of the kids in town were already scared of Bertha and Bartleby, and that gave them a certain amount of power. But if Magnus could convince everyone that he alone controlled B&B . . . that he was the only person standing between their nightsticks and your face . . . well, that would make him the *most* powerful, wouldn't it?

Bartleby released the weeping boy to Eliza Johanssen, his cousin. Eliza shot *Jean* a look of loathing, and Jean's pitcher trembled in her hands. If she had just done her job and poured the tea instead of needling Magnus, none of this would have happened.

"Here." She reached for the boy's empty cup. "I'm sorry you had to wait."

A bowl of porridge and an omelet were waiting for Jean when she returned to the kitchen. She scarfed them down as Isara bent over the griddle, scraping burnt-on egg. She hadn't eaten since last night's cream cheese and gumdrop sandwich, and she had never tasted a breakfast so good. The pork bits in the omelet were especially savory and delicious.

"Did you eat?" she asked Isara between huge mouthfuls.

"Later," he said. "Did you bus the dirty dishes?"

"Bus?"

"Pick them up, put them through the dishwasher. We need them clean for lunch."

"Oh. I'll get on that right away."

Isara grunted and turned back to his scraping. Jean

dropped her dishes into the sink, then spotted her coat hanging behind the door.

She glanced over her shoulder; Isara was still busy. Reading Dr. Fields's paper would only take a minute. She crossed the room and pulled out the crumpled sheet.

Warning: Thistleberry Toxicity!

Citizens of St. Polonius: My laboratory work has recently isolated a neurotoxin that exists in trace amounts in thistleberries. When consumed in small quantities—as in the traditional jams and cordials St. Polonian families have been making at home for centuries—the substance elicits only the most mild, and temporary, soporific effect.

However, producing thistleberry products on an industrial scale will repeatedly expose handlers to this toxin, resulting in potentially deleterious effects to their health, such as extended stupor and possibly even coma. While I am working to formulate an antidote, it has not yet been tested. Therefore, I urge you to

VOTE NO on October 21

Yours in science,
Mary Fields, PhD
Professor of Biochemistry
Great Northern University—
St. Polonius-on-the-Fjord Extension

Soporific? Deleterious? Magnus would have a field day making a spelling test out of this document. Maybe he was right—there were certain vocabulary words you should know if you wanted to be a scientist.

Jean did understand *coma*, though. Could this have something to do with the hibernation?

The last time Jean had helped out at the lab, Dr. Fields had made her put on protective gloves and eyewear because they were extracting . . . something . . . from a thistleberry. Jean hadn't thought it strange—Dr. Fields always took precautions. But this time, she must have made a dangerous discovery: a "neurotoxin." Which made her want to tell everyone to VOTE NO.

"Jean! The dishes?"

Jean stuffed the paper back into her coat pocket. She'd show it to Katrin later, and they'd figure out what to do next.

Welcome to

Ye Olde Mill Inn

Burt Miller, Proprietor

Serving the finest in traditional
St. Polonian cuisine since 1792

CHAPTER 14

One downside of the now-well-behaved dining room was that it was too quiet to pull Katrin aside at lunchtime without someone noticing. Katrin was still able to sit with Micah, at least—like the Huddys, she didn't have any local family. But now Axel Gorson was sitting with them, too.

"Aren't you supposed to eat with your relatives?" Jean scowled at him as she plunked down bowls of rice and lamb curry. "Those Marx kids are your cousins."

"Can't," Axel said through a mouth already stuffed with rice. "Excommunicated."

"What?"

"They don't talk to him anymore since he ran into the little one's foot with his bike last year," Katrin said. "Fractured the kid's toe."

"Typical," Jean muttered.

"I said he could sit with us, Jeannie," Micah said quietly. "I know you're mad about the ride in the plow—I was, too. But Axel *is* my friend. And if he sits with me, I can make sure he doesn't cause more trouble. I don't want him to get whacked by B&B."

So kind—that was Micah. Jean ruffled his already messy hair.

He ducked away, and she laughed. "Hey, you could use a trim!"

A wily smile crossed Katrin's lips. They were deep pink; she must have raided her mom's makeup case that morning. "Speaking of trims," she said, "Gorson, my mom's appointment book has your dad down for a haircut today. I assume you'll be taking his place?"

Axel hardly looked up from his lunch. "Huh?"

Katrin's smirk grew wider. "According to the town charter,

we're all supposed to fulfill our parents' obligations. And an appointment is an obligation—wouldn't you say so, Jean?"

"Oh, definitely."

Axel stopped chewing and ran a hand through his precious long hair. "Um . . ."

"Great." Katrin shot Jean a wink. "I'll see you in the salon at one o'clock."

After the lunch rush, Jean had a chance to try Isara's curry herself. Wow! It had peanuts, potatoes, and tender chunks of lamb in a creamy sauce. She had never had a dish made with coconut milk before. This curry made her wish she could have it at every meal.

Isara, though, ate a bowl of plain rice. "Sometimes, when I spend too long working on a dish, I lose my appetite for it," he said.

Finished eating, Jean pulled off her bandana, tossed it onto the coatrack, and slumped against the kitchen wall. She would have loved to sit down, but there wasn't a chair in the kitchen—and if she did, she might never stand up again. How did Isara's parents do this all day, every day?

"What are you doing?" Isara asked.

Jean's eyelids, which had started drooping, snapped open. "I'm resting," she told him. "Ever heard of it?"

"Resting?"

"Yes." Jean flexed her aching back. "Try it sometime."

Isara slid a tray of bowls into the dishwasher and slapped the cage down over it. The machine hummed and sloshed loudly.

"There's no time for resting," he said. "First course for tonight's dinner will be tom yum soup. We have to start peeling the shrimps, because the stock needs to boil for at least an hour."

"First course?" Jean asked, incredulous. "How many courses are you planning?"

"Well, it is dinner," Isara said. "So, three."

Jean balked. "Didn't you say you don't have enough ingredients to last the whole winter? Why don't we make something simpler? Most of these kids would probably be happy with a sandwich, you know?"

"Do you mean serve a cold dinner?" Isara looked appalled. "In this weather? My parents would never allow that!"

"But your parents aren't in charge," Jean said. "You are. Your food is delicious, but if you keep making these fancy dishes for every meal, you're going to burn out in a week. Maybe less. *I'm* already keeling over."

"I have to do my best," Isara said. "For my parents' sake."

"I get it," Jean said. "You want to make them proud—"

But Isara shook his head. "It's not just that. A lot of these kids have never had Thai food before. If, at the end of the winter, they love it, they'll come back with their families. Business will take off. And then maybe, in a few years, we'll have saved enough to shut down."

"You want the restaurant to do well . . . so it can go out of business?"

The dishwasher buzzed, its cycle over. "I know it sounds strange," Isara said, unloading. "But my parents don't want to cook forever. They were marine biologists in Thailand. They wanted to come here to study whales. But there's not much money in that, and the Thai government will support people who open restaurants in other countries . . . so here we are."

"Huh." Jean had never really thought about what had brought Isara's family halfway around the world. They'd come for scientific reasons, like Dr. Fields. Thistleberries only grew on this side of the fjord, so Dr. Fields couldn't do her research anywhere else.

"When everyone wakes up," Jean said, "I want your parents to meet Dr. Mary Fields at the university. She might be able to help them get back into the world of science. She's very encouraging—she lets me help out in her lab all the time."

Isara put the last clean plate back in the cupboard. "Thanks, Jean. That would be great."

"But in the meantime," Jean said, "give yourself a break. I vote sandwiches for dinner."

Isara sighed. "That would be nice," he said, "but there's no bread or sandwich fillings in our pantry. Only Thai ingredients."

"True," Jean said, "but there's the general store. Oh—and Ye Olde Mill Inn! It's shut down, because Mr. Miller doesn't have any kids to run it for him. But we shouldn't let his supplies go to waste, should we? If we raid the inn's stock, we can probably get at least a few days' worth of food to serve the kids—maybe even a few weeks'!"

Isara cocked his head. He was probably thinking of their

fishing expedition, and whether he should trust Jean to lead another quest.

"It'll be easy—the restaurant's just a block away. We'll grab what we need and go."

"All right," he agreed. "Let's see what's in the inn's pantry."

The snow was still falling when they stepped out the kitchen door. And a mob of kids was blocking Skiff Alley, crowded around the window of Ash Beauty & Tattoo Parlor.

"Shave! Shave!" they chanted.

Jean pushed her way to the front of the crowd. In the salon, covered in a sheet and looking absolutely terrified, sat Axel; behind him Katrin was happily buzzing all the hair off the left side of his head.

"Yeahhh!" the mob cheered, and Katrin, holding her electric razor out like it was a bouquet of flowers, curtsied.

"*What* is going on here?" Bertha Smuthers shouted. The kids in the alley shrank back.

Bartleby was close behind. "Back to work, all of you!"

Most of the younger kids ran off. But a few older ones were brave enough to stick around.

"I *can't* work," nine-year-old Jack Perigee said. "My dad's a fisherman, but he'd never take a boat out in weather like this."

"Yeah—and no one's come into the general store all morning," Jillian Seidel-Mitchell complained. She was ten. "Am I just supposed to sit around in there all day?"

"These are questions for the mayor," Bartleby said. "You can make an appointment with his assistant to see him at town hall."

"I tried," Jack said, "but Liddy said he was out this afternoon, and she didn't know when he was coming back."

Out of the office? What was Magnus up to now?

"Jack," Bartleby said, "I command you to go shopping for new tackle at Jill's store. That way, you'll have something to do, and she'll have a customer. Problem solved."

But Jack didn't seem to think so. "I don't *need* new tackle. And if my dad wakes up and finds out I spent his money—"

"Will he be happier to wake up and learn that you got arrested for loitering in Skiff Alley?" Bertha leaned over him. "Now get lost."

Jillian grabbed Jack's elbow. "It's okay," she murmured as they left together. "You don't have to pay me in money—I'll take chocolate."

"Come on," Isara whispered to Jean, "before they arrest *us*." They slipped out of Skiff Alley, past the corner where Axel's snowplow was parked at a crazy angle.

Ye Olde Mill Inn had the best location in town for a restaurant, a tall building with views out over the fjord. Years back, when St. Polonius had gotten a trickle of summer tourists, it had been busier. But with the rise of Bigsby, the Inn's business had suffered, along with its food. With only locals to feed, Mr. Miller didn't make much of an effort. The one time Jean had come, she'd barely made it through her overcooked salmon burger.

Jean had a hunch that Isara could do better with Mr. Miller's ingredients—*if* they could get them. The front door of the restaurant was shut tight.

"Let me try," Isara said, but they heard a bolt rattling inside.

Paranoid Mr. Miller! Jean thought. St. Polonius wasn't a door-locking kind of town, but the inn's owner had always been odd, muttering about teenage "hoodlums" and government conspiracies. He had even once accused a pair of backpackers of being scouts for a Bigsby restaurant, trying to steal his recipes. He'd kicked them right out of Ye Olde Mill Inn.

No wonder visitors never came to St. Polonius anymore.

"Kitchen door?" Isara asked.

Jean nodded.

They circled the building, the snow growing much deeper as soon as they left the plowed street out front. Even the huge garbage bins were all but buried.

The kitchen door was locked.

Isara groaned. "We've wasted valuable cooking time. I need to get back and start on the soup."

"Hold on," Jean said. "A window . . . up there! Come on, give me a boost."

Isara sighed, but cupped his gloved hands together. Jean braced herself against his shoulders, stuck her boot into the step he'd created, and sprang up toward the window, which was a good six feet off the ground. She shoved hard at the glass and it budged.

She jumped back down. "I think I can get it open, I just need a little more time. Could I sit up on your shoulders? Then I'd be able to reach it easily."

Isara knelt and motioned for Jean to climb aboard. He

felt steady under her when he stood; soccer must have given him strong legs.

When she looked into the restaurant, Jean was surprised to see a light on in the kitchen—and then, movement.

Someone else was already inside Ye Olde Mill Inn.

CHAPTER 15

“Is it opening?” Isara called.

“Shhh!” Jean pressed her nose closer to the window. A kid wrapped in a long black cloak was dragging a box across the kitchen floor—a large box with a triangle-shaped symbol stamped on the outside. His or her face was hidden by a balaclava.

“Someone’s in there!” she hissed.

“Good! Ask them to let us in!”

"Just a minute." If someone was inside, why were both of the doors locked? What was this kid up to?

Jean watched as the figure pulled open a large silver door, like the one to the walk-in refrigerator at the Tasty Thai Hut. The kid dragged the box inside, came out without it, and headed for the door beside Jean.

"Put me down!" she cried. "Fast!"

Isara was quick, and Jean pitched headfirst into a snowdrift. She scrambled to her feet, shoving snow out of her face, and yanked Isara behind a garbage bin as the kitchen door swung open. The mysterious kid stepped outside, looked both ways, and ducked around the corner of the building.

Jean hurtled out of her hiding place and sprinted through the snow to the door. Hurling herself the final few feet, she got the toe of her boot into the doorway before it slammed shut.

"Wow!" Isara slogged through the snow behind her and grabbed the door's handle. "You must *really* like sandwiches."

"Yeah—sandwiches," Jean gasped. "Worth risking life and limb for."

Inside, they flipped on the light switch. It was a larger, brighter space than the Tasty Thai Hut's kitchen, but somehow less cheerful. Isara flung open an enormous deep freezer chest. "Look!" he cried. "Packed with fish fillets." He lifted a great slab up to show Jean. "Sea bass," he said. "An open-ocean fish. I didn't know they could be caught in the fjord."

Jean shrugged. Mr. Miller was known to be a devoted fisherman, setting sail in his motorboat after most local fisherfolk had returned for the day, and staying out well past sunset. Who knew what he managed to catch?

If Isara was happy to find the sea bass, then she was happy for him. "I'm going to check out the refrigerator," she said. "Whoever that was in the kitchen left something in there. The box had a big triangle on it."

When Jean opened the refrigerator door, a light flicked on revealing shelves filled with food. The nearest one held jars of pickled turnips, horseradish, and stewed prunes.

Blech! No wonder no one wanted to eat here anymore.

The next shelf was packed with cardboard boxes, but none had the triangle symbol. The rear shelves held loaves of bread and wedges of sheep-cheese from her own farm. In frustration, she kicked the wall beside the cheese shelf—and felt it rattle against her boot.

A door! Jean gave it a hard shove, and it creaked open.

The temperature plummeted as she stepped into this new, darker room—a walk-in freezer. Another light flicked on overhead, and Jean blinked as her eyes adjusted.

She gasped.

The shelf right in front of her held row after row of triangular fins, the edge of each one rust colored with blood where it had been hacked from a shark's body. A stew made with shark fins had been a St. Polonian delicacy long ago—people's grandparents talked about having eaten it in their youth. But slaughtering sharks for their fins had been illegal for decades.

Jean glanced up to a higher shelf that was packed with enormous, plastic-wrapped hunks of a dark red meat. She stretched to read a sticker on one of the packages; a date from only a couple of months ago, and a single word: *whale.*

You could go to jail for years for hunting or eating a whale. This freezer was hidden for a reason.

Shaking slightly, Jean finally spotted the cardboard box with the triangle shoved in under the lowest shelf. She took a deep breath of icy freezer air. What fresh horror would she find inside? Endangered falcon corpses? The head of a baby narwhal?

She crouched low and fumbled at the box with her mittens. Inside: two jumbo-size plastic baggies—one nearly empty, and the other packed full of a grayish-brown substance. Jean pulled a hand out of its mitten and, cringing slightly, gave the full bag a poke. The substance gave way easily to her finger's pressure. It hadn't had time to start freezing yet.

It looked familiar. Where had she seen it before?

"Jean?" Isara stood in the freezer doorway. "What is this place?"

"I'm not sure . . . but this is the box that that kid left. Trying to hide it in here, I think."

Isara knelt down. "The bear liver. From the festival."

"That's it!" Jean cried. "Yes, of course! But . . . why is there so much of it left over?"

"Maybe more than one bear sacrificed its liver this year?"

Jean shook her head. "The mayor only allows the killing of one bear per year for Founders' Day—that's why everyone only gets one bite of liver, so there'll be enough to go around. There's never any extra . . . at least, I don't think so. But even if there was, why would someone want to hide it?"

"I don't know," Isara said, "but look. Something's written on the other side of this bag."

LOW-ALTITUDE BEAR LIVER

Tested, 13 October, by Dr. Mary Fields

Jean looked at the label on the other bag.

HIGH-ALTITUDE BEAR LIVER

Tested, 13 October, by Dr. Mary Fields

And *that* was the bag that was almost empty.

"Do not serve?" Jean said. "But . . . why?"

"This doesn't seem good."

"No," she agreed. "Someone must have switched the bags at the festival . . . and now their kid is trying to cover it up by hiding the leftovers in here!"

Isara looked skeptical, but Jean was sure she was right. This was where Mr. Miller hid things he didn't want inspectors to find. The question was, who else knew about it?

"Who is Mr. Miller friendly with?" she wondered.

"That nasty old man?" Isara asked. "I would guess no one. When my parents first opened their restaurant, he filed several complaints at town hall, trying to get it shut down. We got letters accusing us of code violations—all lies."

"That's awful," Jean said. It sounded like exactly the sort

of thing Mr. Miller would do, though. And sharing the location of his secret freezer sounded like something Mr. Miller would *never* do, since it was full of evidence that could send him to jail.

Unless, of course, he'd shared it with someone who could promise he wouldn't be arrested. Someone who had control over the police.

"The mayor!" Jean blurted. "And . . . and Magnus!"

Isara gave her a curious look. "What about them?"

Jean's brain was racing. The Kings were mixed up in this somehow. And everyone who had eaten the liver labeled DO NOT SERVE had gone into hibernation. Everyone but Isara—unless, like her, he was hiding something.

If it turned out that both she *and* Isara hadn't eaten their liver . . . well, she was willing to admit it if he was.

Jean looked him straight in the eye. "Isara, did you really eat the liver on Founders' Day?"

The color faded from his cheeks. "What?"

"Please, I just . . . I need to know the truth."

He took a step backward into the refrigerator. "You're suspicious of me? Because I'm a foreigner?"

"What? No!"

"You're acting just like *he* does."

"Like who?"

"*Magnus,*" Isara spat, and Jean cringed. He was right. She'd sounded like she was accusing him of something—exactly what Magnus had done to *her* that morning.

"Isara, I didn't mean it that way."

He glared at her. "Then don't ask me again."

"I—I won't."

He nodded sharply. "Then let's start collecting what we can use from this refrigerator. Okay?" He grabbed a loaf of bread.

Good job, Jean! she thought. She hadn't gotten the information she needed, and she'd hurt Isara's feelings trying. She kicked the stamped box at her feet—but then crouched down and snatched the almost-empty bag of DO NOT SERVE liver out of it. Crumpling it into a ball, she stuffed it into her coat pocket beside Dr. Fields's paper.

Evidence. She closed the box and pushed it back under the shelf.

Evidence of what, though? She had no idea.

BORED WITH YOUR JOB?

Lots of extra time on your hands?
Want to earn more pocket money?

An exciting new opportunity may
await you in . . . POLICE WORK!

The St. Polonius Police Force is seeking new recruits to work for the town on a part-time basis in the fields of surveillance and security. Help make sure that everyone in town obeys the law!

To schedule your police-work spelling aptitude test (administered by Interim Mayor Magnus King), please make an appointment with Liddy Dowell at town hall.

CHAPTER 16

When Jean returned to Katrin's that night, Micah was already in bed, snuggled up next to Rambo and snoring lightly.

"Hi, honey!" Katrin called from the kitchen table. "How was your day?"

The table was covered with money—bills and coins divided into neat stacks. "What's all this?" Jean asked.

"My earnings," Katrin said. "After my demo with Axel, kids are lining up for my services! I worked on all five

Hansens this afternoon, and their cousins are booked tomorrow. I guess everyone figures it's time to get the wild haircuts of their dreams. I have to study up on my straight razor technique tonight."

"That's great." Jean tried to sound thrilled.

Katrin smiled. "Thanks. Mom's going to be so happy when she wakes up. I'm making everyone pay me in real money—none of this 'work for candy' codwash! At this rate, I'll be able to save up enough to buy this cool color-mixer: the Inkmaster 3000. Only two salons in the capital have one. We'd be the first in the north, even ahead of Bigsby."

Bigsby! Had Jean tried to sail there only that morning? So much had happened since. "I have a lot to tell you."

As she spoke, Katrin's black-rimmed eyes grew wider and wider. "You tried to cross the fjord?" she gasped. "And Magnus *tricked* you into working at the Tasty Thai Hut? And you found a mysterious paper in Dr. Fields's pocket? *And* there's a secret freezer full of whale and shark parts and liver at Ye Olde Mill Inn? Jean, this is all—crazy!"

Jean pulled out the near-empty bag of high-altitude liver and the paper she had found on Dr. Fields that morning. She plunked them onto the table. "So what do you think of all this?"

Katrin examined the bag of liver. "Well, it says DO NOT SERVE . . . but it doesn't say why."

"Exactly," Jean said. "Which is why it's such a mystery!"

"Maybe it's not a big deal," Katrin said. "Maybe it hadn't been refrigerated properly before, and it went bad before Dr. Fields tested it. How did it taste when you ate it?"

"Disgusting." The memory made Jean wince. "And my dad thought so, too."

"Well, there you go. It was probably a little off, but you all ate it anyway because you're upright citizens of St. Polonius, and that's what we do. I can't wait until I get to taste it next year."

Jean swallowed hard. The one thing she hadn't told Katrin about was how Magnus had hinted that she hadn't eaten her liver, and threatened to punish her if he found proof. What would Katrin think if she learned the truth?

"Honestly," Katrin continued, "I'd be more concerned about this paper of Dr. Fields's than about the liver. One bite of spoiled liver can't make you that sick—but she makes thistleberries sound dangerous!"

"Let's find out for sure," Jean said, and Katrin nodded. She rummaged through the bookshelf and returned with a plump dictionary. The girls looked up all the words they didn't know.

"So," Katrin said, "she's saying she's discovered that big amounts of thistleberries can make you . . . drunk?"

"Or worse." Jean examined the paper again. *Soporific:* something that can make you sleepy. *Deleterious:* toxic or dangerous. *Stupor:* a state in which you have no energy. And Dr. Fields said she hadn't yet tested her *antidote:* a cure.

"You don't think," Jean said slowly, "that all the sleepers might have *already* gotten poisoned somehow by thistleberries, do you? That that could have somehow caused their hibernation?"

Katrin shook her head. "She says here that the amount

we normally eat in relish and tea and stuff doesn't do much damage . . . and that's all anyone would have had on Founders' Day, right?"

Jean nodded. She'd had tea and jam on Founders' Day, and she was fine.

Katrin continued. "But Dr. Fields is concerned that processing big amounts of thistleberries in a plant could be dangerous for workers and have bad long-term effects."

"And that's why her paper says to vote no on October twenty-first."

"Exactly—though it's weird that you only found one of them on her." Katrin picked up the paper again. "It looks like a flyer—like she had it printed up to pass out to people at the festival. You didn't see any more in her coat?"

"No. But who knows—she could have lost them in the mayhem of the hibernation." *Or,* Jean thought, *a kid could have disposed of them once everyone was asleep.*

"I wish Magnus had let you take over Dr. Fields's job, like you asked," Katrin said. "Especially since she made such an important discovery! The other kids in town should have this information, don't you think? Better satellites would be good, but if processing thistleberries can make people sick, then no one will want to vote yes on the proposal next week." She stroked a teased lock of hair thoughtfully. "I mean, our parents are already sick enough. I wouldn't want my mom to start working at a toxic factory right after she woke up from a coma."

"Me neither," Jean said. If she couldn't wake her parents, then the least she could do was protect them from having to take jobs they didn't want in a factory that could make them sick all over again. She had to make sure that the thistleberry measure failed in the election next week.

"It's lucky you found the flyer," Katrin was saying, "because now we can spread the word. What do you think we should do? Take it to Magnus the Magnificent and ask him to make an announcement?"

Jean shook her head vigorously. Passing the thistleberry plant measure had been Mayor Theobald King's goal for the last six months. Magnus would carry out his father's mission, no matter what.

And he wouldn't believe any evidence *she* brought him anyway.

"We can't trust Magnus," Jean said. "Not with how strictly he's been following the town charter, and definitely not after he tricked me today with that test. How'd he even know I hadn't gone back to the farm when he sent B&B to pick me up? Do you think he has kids spying for him, checking that people are doing their jobs?"

"If he doesn't, he will soon." Katrin pulled a flyer of her own out of her back pocket. "He and his crew were passing these around at dinner. He wants more police."

Jean read the flyer. "Great—another dozen Berthas and Bartlebys running around with nightsticks!"

"I wonder what words he'll put on that spelling test," Katrin mused. "*Law? Order?*"

"*Threats? Beatings?*"

"Let's hope it doesn't go that far."

"If he's starting up a serious spy force," Jean said, "then that's all the more reason to spread the word about the thistleberry danger on our own. You know, quietly."

"Quietly, like how you snuck off to Bigsby this morning without telling anyone?" Katrin grinned. "A whisper campaign? Fine by me. Any ideas on how to start?"

Jean thought for a moment. "Dr. Fields's office is right next to my dad's—I mean, Micah's. I can stop by tomorrow and see if I can find any more copies of her flyer, or any other evidence from her research that would help us. Then maybe we can hand the flyers out and explain things to the kids ourselves. You can do that when they come in for haircuts, right?"

"Sure," Katrin said. "And you can do it when you serve meals."

"We're on," Jean said, and she reached across a pile of money to squeeze her best friend's hand.

It felt good to have a plan.

CHAPTER 17

Walking into the restaurant's kitchen the following morning, Jean was greeted by a blast of humid air and the musky scent of steaming shellfish.

"Isara," she groaned, tossing her coat onto the rack, "I thought we agreed, no more fancy breakfasts! Where are those boxes of cereal we took from Ye Olde Mill Inn?"

Isara looked up from the counter, where he was shelling shrimp and tossing them into a pot. "But we took all these extra shrimp from the Mill Inn, too! I'm making my father's breakfast specialty, khao tom; it's a soup of seafood, vegetables, and rice. It's not that much work."

He's a lost cause, Jean thought—and she also wondered how the kids out in the dining room would feel about eating seafood soup for breakfast. The omelets and rice porridge had gone over pretty well yesterday, but they weren't so different from the eggs and oatmeal kids usually ate at home.

Jean opened her mouth to say this but thought better of it. At least Isara was talking to her. After the incident in Mr. Miller's freezer yesterday, they'd barely spoken. Isara had even left Jean alone to make dinner sandwiches while he joined a snow soccer game on the square (after making her swear not to touch the stove or open any cans while he was gone).

Jean made the tea. When the soup was ready, she took the first tray of bowls and headed to the dining room.

As she stepped out of the kitchen, though, she nearly dropped her tray.

The dining room walls had been decorated with three beautiful wooden hangings. Isara had told her they were hand carved by his grandfather in Thailand, the only pieces of art his parents had taken with them when they'd moved across the world.

But today the hangings were stashed in a corner, replaced by scribbled posters. One showed a bunch of red ovals clustered together with a green sprig shooting out from the top; a second featured a smiling stick-figure family with the caption *We like thizleberys!* The last one showed a picture of a TV set, with the words *Thiztelbarie plant meanz more TV chanlez!*

Thistleberry plant means more TV channels.

Jean's ears started to burn. Isara would *never* have taken his grandfather's art down. Someone had removed the carvings and hung these posters without permission . . . and she knew who it was.

She stormed toward the mayor's table. The kids at the day-care center must have made these. But she doubted the messages on the posters were their own ideas.

Magnus was staring at the posters, too—and he looked as unhappy as Jean. "Misspellings!" he hissed at Amelia. "I gave you specific wording. How hard is it to get kids to copy letters?"

Amelia quaked in her seat. "I'm s-sorry, Mr. Mayor," she stammered. "The children—they're little, and some of them don't even know the alphabet yet. . . ."

Now Jean was thrilled that Isara had made soup for breakfast. She plunked her steaming bowls down onto the table, letting hot liquid slosh over the sides.

"Watch it!" Bertha snapped. Bartleby glared at Jean, too, but Magnus was preoccupied.

"I want these fixed," he told Amelia. "I want them taken down, and—"

"Here, let me help you with that." Jean reached behind Amelia, yanked the nearest poster off the wall, and plunged it into the puddle of spilled soup.

Suddenly, everyone at the table was on their feet.

"Wait!"

"Stop!"

"What are you doing?"

But Jean kept wiping soup with the poster, watching its paper disintegrate and the magic marker on it melt into rainbow-colored swirls.

Bartleby banged a fist on the table. "Waitress, you've destroyed a day-care student's art project! Explain yourself!"

"Oh, was that art?" Jean asked innocently. "I just knew that it didn't belong on this restaurant's walls, so I assumed it was trash."

Bertha was snorting like a horse, nostrils flaring. "Of course it belongs on these walls! Ms. Willoughby's students created these for public display, with the mayor's approval. And what place is more public than the restaurant where everyone eats their meals?"

"Just because the public comes in here doesn't mean that this isn't a private establishment, *Constable,*" Jean retorted. "And the *mayor,*" she continued, turning to Magnus, "being so familiar with all the laws of this town, should certainly know that."

Jean was a bit surprised to hear herself talking so forcefully to him. But if nobody else was willing to call Magnus out on his mistakes, she would have to do it.

Smiling calmly, Magnus looked up at Jean. "Ms. Huddy is right. I want the rest of these posters removed—permanently."

All around the table, jaws dropped.

"But, Mr. Mayor," Liddy cried, "what about the campaign? The vote on the thistleberry plant is next week!"

"Then we'll find other ways to share our message," Magnus said. "Relying on the labor of toddlers was a beginner's mistake. Thank you, Ms. Huddy, for making that abundantly clear."

Jean blinked. "Uh . . . you're welcome." Was Magnus actually grateful? He flashed a grin at her, but his eyes were as cold as two blue pieces of fjord ice.

"Well, please rehang the carvings, and be careful with them," Jean instructed the table. When she turned away, she spotted Isara in the kitchen doorway. He watched as Bartleby lifted the first hanging back up onto the wall, then he turned to Jean and nodded.

She nodded back, but her triumph was short-lived.

"Did you see what that poster said?" she heard ten-year-old Minnie Payne asking her table. "More TV channels if we vote yes on the thistleberry plant! Because then the town will have money for better satellites."

"And that means faster Internet, too," her younger brother added. "Games all year round! I'm voting yes."

These kids needed more information—now. Jean had to get her hands on more of Dr. Fields's flyers.

The local branch of Great Northern University was a squat brown building at the far west end of town. The main campus in the capital was much larger and nicer; Jean's dad had taken the family down there once for a conference. Jean had vivid memories of red-brick buildings connected by green lawns, and a great domed library filled to the top with books.

The St. Polonius outpost had no real campus or library. Lectures were held either at town hall or in the church, and textbooks, which had to be ordered by mail, often arrived weeks into the semester. But at least each professor had his or her own office in the drafty Extension building. For the past five years, Dad had been neighbors with Dr. Fields.

Jean let herself in through the creaky door and shivered, wondering whether it was possible for a building to be colder inside than it was outside. As she moved down the hallway, she passed other offices that had been taken over by professors' children. On the floor of the classics office, nine-year-old Pete Rudberg was building an enormous castle out of *Odysseys* and *Aeneids*, while several kids were clustered in the math department, making airplanes out of graph paper. A series of loud bangs came from the physics lab; Jean didn't want to know what was going on in there.

The door to Dad's office was wide open, and Jean found Micah bouncing a rubber ball toward Rambo, who sat in the corner.

"C'mon, boy! Catch the ball! Catch the— No, Rambo, don't *chew* it!"

Micah scrambled forward and grabbed the ball. Rambo let out a *baaah!*

"Jeannie!" Micah spotted his sister. "Wanna play ball? Rambo's not so good at catch."

"I'd love to," Jean said, "but I can't stay. I told Isara I'd be back in half an hour to help with lunch."

Micah wore one of Dad's tweed jackets—the one he left

at the office—but it actually didn't look that big on Micah since he was still wearing his winter coat underneath.

"It's freezing in here, isn't it?" Jean asked.

"Yeah, something's wrong with the heating—it's at half power."

"What?" Jean cried. "Then it's not safe for you kids to be working in here! And there don't seem to be any students around for you to teach anyway."

Micah bounced his ball and caught it in his other hand. "Yeah—all of us professors' kids got together yesterday to talk about that. Turns out no one who's enrolled in the university has a kid old enough to take their classes for them, so none of us have teaching to do. Mayor Magnus said we should do our parents' research, but we don't understand it. The kids working here are getting bored. . . . I think some of them are gonna apply for that police job instead."

"Great," Jean groaned.

Micah shrugged. "Pete told Mayor Magnus about the problem with the heat yesterday at dinner," he said, "and this morning the daughter of the regular repair person showed up."

"That's good, I guess."

"Yeah," Micah said, "but she's only seven, so she wasn't able to do much. I tried to help her, since I'm good with tools, but I'm more of an inventor than a fixer, ya know?"

Jean grinned, thinking of Rambo's snowshoes. "Yeah, I know."

"Anyway," Micah said, "the kettle still works, so we all

take turns making cocoa and bringing it around the office every hour. We've got a schedule up on the whiteboard and everything! It'll be my turn at three. But . . ." He sighed.

"What is it?"

Micah bounced the ball again. "I wish I was working on the farm, you know? Hey, maybe I can ask Magnus for a special job switch, like you did. What do you think?"

"You could ask," Jean said, "but it's gonna be pretty snowed-in at this point, and we know that the automatic systems can take care of the animals for weeks. And even if you did make it back, we'd be separated, with no way to contact each other."

"Then forget it," Micah said. "I want to stay here in town. With you."

In spite of the cold office, Micah's words warmed Jean from the inside out. She would keep him close—keep him safe.

"So what are you doing here?" he asked.

"Oh—I want to look around Dr. Fields's office. She might have made a pretty major discovery about thistleberries, information Katrin and I think the kids in town should have before the vote next week."

"Cool," Micah said. "Can I help? What is it you're looking for?"

"I'm not sure," she said. "Let's see what we can find."

Jean gave Rambo a pat on her way into the hall. Dr. Fields's office was right next door—but it was locked. Jean rattled the doorknob, but the office was shut up tighter than a greedy oyster clamped over a pearl.

In all the times she'd visited her dad's office, Jean had never known any of the professors to lock their doors. Whenever Dr. Fields had invited her to the lab to help out, Jean had walked right in.

Had Dr. Fields locked her door on purpose before heading out to the Founders' Day celebration? Was there something in there she wanted to protect?

Jean asked Micah to have a crack at the door, since he was better at solving mechanical problems. He tried jimmying the lock with a paper clip from Dad's desk. No luck. Meanwhile, the other young "professors" started to pop into the hall.

Jean touched Micah's shoulder. "Let's not do this while people are looking," she whispered. "I can come back tomorrow—maybe the salon has tools we can use."

Micah nodded.

But when Jean returned the next day, something much worse than a lock barred the door to Dr. Fields's lab: Bertha and Bartleby Smuthers.

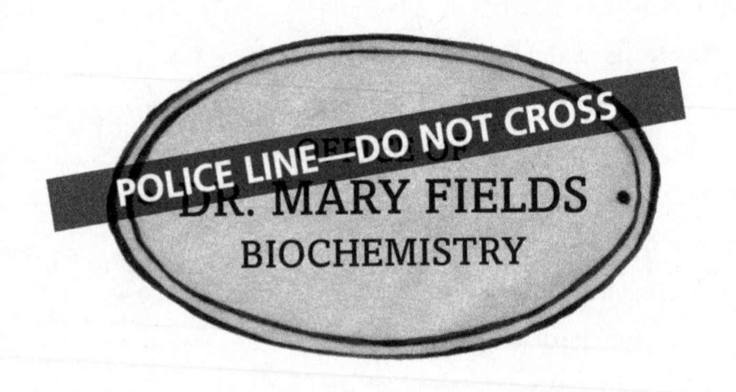

CHAPTER 18

"Greetings, Waitress Huddy," Bartleby said. He and Bertha were sitting on folding chairs in front of the door, clutching paper cups of cocoa. "Are you looking for your brother's office? It's next door."

"I know where his office is, thanks." The tools Jean had borrowed from Katrin's shop clinked loudly in her backpack. "Um, what are you doing here?"

Bertha sat up straighter. "We received a report yesterday that someone was trying to break into Dr. Fields's lab."

One of the other "professors" must have squealed—and had probably been rewarded with an exciting new job. At breakfast, several kids wearing shiny police badges had cluttered up their tables with slingshots, water guns, and other weapons. A few even carried toy harpoons from Founders' Day.

"It's our duty to protect the property of citizens of St. Polonius-on-the-Fjord," Bartleby said. "Even the sleeping ones."

"So we're guarding this door." Bertha gave Jean a shrewd look. "*You* wouldn't happen to have any information about the break-in attempt, would you?"

"Who, me? No way." Jean took a step backward. Bertha knew exactly who had been at that door, and was playing stupid. "Well . . . Micah seems pretty busy, so I guess I'll head back to work myself. Good luck with your stakeout, or whatever it is." Jean forced herself to walk back down the hallway slowly, despite her urge to flee.

B&B knew she'd been snooping—which meant Magnus knew. That couldn't be good.

Jean cornered Katrin in the alley after lunch and told her in a whisper what had happened.

"They're guarding the door?" Katrin whispered back. "*Both* of them?"

Jean nodded.

"I wonder if Magnus knows about Dr. Fields's research," Katrin said, "and doesn't want anyone finding it. You saw the posters he put up yesterday, campaigning *for* the thistleberry plant."

"I know," Jean said. Bertha and Bartleby had missed lunch—still at Dr. Fields's door, she supposed—but Magnus had huddled up with Pastor Kris, Secretary Liddy, and Day Care Coordinator Amelia. What were they plotting now?

That night, as she emerged from the kitchen with Isara's goose-meat pad thai, Jean noticed that the mayor's table was occupied by a family of kids who usually sat on the floor.

She spotted Magnus with a different family in the far corner. He was passing out the pink candies from his desk at town hall as he spoke.

Amelia sat in another circle of siblings. And Kris was with a different group. Jean moved in close to hear him.

"All right, confession time. Tell me the truth—do you like doing your parents' jobs?"

"I do!" Jean recognized the speaker as the little boy B&B had threatened at breakfast the other day. "It's fun to use my dad's power tools. He never let me touch them before."

"Yeah," agreed his cousin Eliza. "Working at the library is way more fun than school. I get to read whatever books I want—even romances!"

The other kids said they liked their new jobs, too.

"Good," Kris said. "But of course, when the grown-ups wake up, it'll be back to the old system. *Unless* . . ." He paused dramatically. "Oh, never mind."

He had the kids hooked like a school of gaping codfish. "Unless what?" Eliza squeaked.

"Well," Kris continued, "if a thistleberry processing plant gets built in St. Polonius, we'll need people to work there. Adults—like your parents." He turned to the first boy who had spoken. "And when your dad is busy working his shift at the plant, well, who'll fill in at his old job? It'll have to be someone with experience. Someone like . . ."

"Me!" the boy cried.

"Exactly," said Kris. "And the same goes for all the rest of you. So if we all vote YES next week in the big election . . ."

". . . we'll get to keep doing our new jobs sometimes!" Eliza finished. "Cool!" The kids around her nodded.

As Jean circled the room, she heard almost the exact same words from Amelia and Magnus. Steam rose from her platter of pad thai, but it could have been coming out of her ears.

One of the only groups that didn't have someone from Team Thistleberry Plant sitting with it was Micah, Axel, and Katrin. Jean headed to their small table by the door. "Have you heard what they're saying? To all the kids?" she fumed.

"Oh, yeah," Katrin replied. "That Liddy girl tried to give us the speech, but we told her to take a hike."

"You did?"

Katrin grabbed a fork and dug into her plate of goose and noodles. "You sound surprised."

"Well," Jean said, "Micah and I don't like our jobs very much, but I know how much you love running the salon."

"Yeah," Micah agreed. "And you love driving your dad's truck, right, Axel?"

To Jean's surprise, Axel shook his recently buzzed head, which now had only a fine, spiky line of hair down the middle. (Katrin's revenge-shaving had totally backfired—he *liked* his new look!)

"Sure, driving is fun for now," he said, "but it's not like I wanna keep this job forever. I've got plans! And driving a plow wouldn't leave a lot of time for me to develop my professional bear-hunting skills."

Katrin snorted. "Professional *what*?"

"Bear. Hunting. You know, hunting bears with weapons and stuff?" A joyful serenity seemed to descend over Axel. "I've gone with my dad—*we* were the ones who hunted the bear whose liver got served on Founders' Day. It's not easy: First you have to track 'em, and that can take a long time. And you've got to start early in the morning, so that wouldn't work with a regular plowing schedule. Dad and I have only gone on his days off."

"Wait," Jean said. "You hunted the bear for Founders' Day?"

"Well, yeah," Axel said. "Why do you think I did such an awesome job acting like a bear in the play? I know their behavior really well."

"Yeah, you did a super-awesome job," Micah said, elbowing Axel in the ribs. "You growled at me so loudly during *The Founders' Story* that I still can't hear out of my left ear!"

"That wasn't a growl!" Axel cried. "It was a defensive roar! Bears make *several* distinct types of sounds: growls, roars, moans, groans. . . ."

Jean turned back to Katrin.

"I've thought a lot about this whole job thing, too," Katrin said in a low voice. "Just because I'm happy following in my mom's footsteps doesn't mean everyone should have to."

Jean grinned at her over the tray of pad thai.

"And especially not now," Katrin continued. "This break is kind of cool, but when my mom wakes up, I know I need to go back to school. She's always saying that I have a lot more to learn if I'm going to become a top stylist one day—art and design, and chemistry. It's kind of a drag . . . but I know she's right." A sudden tear sprang to Katrin's eye. "I miss her, Jean," she whispered. "I never thought I would miss her nagging me."

"I know," Jean whispered back. That was why they needed to defeat the thistleberry plant—so that when their parents did wake up, they could spend time with their kids again and not be stuck in a factory. If Jean wasn't going to get her hands on more of Dr. Fields's flyers or research, they needed a new plan.

"Let's meet at the salon after dinner to brainstorm," Jean whispered. "And fill Micah in . . . and Axel. The more kids we can get on our side, the better."

After dinner, Jean rushed through cleanup. She was shrugging her coat on in the kitchen when Isara stepped up to her, holding a steaming bowl.

"I know you didn't have time to eat," he said, "so I heated this back up for you."

It was such a kind gesture that Jean blushed. "Thanks," she said, "but I have somewhere I need to be."

"Oh." Isara's face fell. "Well, let me pack it up for you. We have plenty of containers."

"Isara," Jean said as he dug around in a cabinet for a box. "Do you like running the restaurant so far?"

"It's fine," he said, his face still in the cabinet. "It's my duty to my parents, and to the town."

"So . . . would you want to keep doing it after they woke up?"

Isara straightened, box in hand. "Why would I do that?"

"Well," Jean said, "you seem good at it, and like you enjoy it, too."

"I do," he said, "but running this restaurant is their job, not mine."

"So you wouldn't want to . . . say . . . send them off to work at a thistleberry processing plant so that you could keep on cooking here?"

"What?" Isara blinked in confusion. "Send my parents to work in a factory so I could steal their business? Who would do such a thing?"

Jean smiled—one more kid for her cause. "Well, you and I wouldn't," she said, "but Magnus and his crew have been suggesting it, and a lot of younger kids seem perfectly willing to vote yes on the thistleberry plant and do just that. And like Magnus said at the schoolhouse meeting, once a measure passes by vote in this town, it's basically impossible to reverse."

"That's terrible," Isara said.

"And that's why we need to do something about it—well, that and the fact that apparently working with thistleberries can be very bad for your health. A few of us are meeting—in secret—to try to come up with a plan. Do you want to come?"

Isara nodded. "Yes!"

"Then grab your coat."

He held up a finger and disappeared back into the walk-in refrigerator. Jean glanced up at the clock on the kitchen wall. "Isara? What are you looking for?"

He reappeared with a cardboard box, smiling. "Snacks. Every first meeting of a secret political opposition group should have snacks."

THE RATANAS' RICE PAPER ROLLS WITH PORK

INGREDIENTS

8 round rice paper wrappers
4 ounces rice vermicelli noodles, cooked & drained
1 cup shredded cooked pork
1 carrot, cut into matchsticks
1/2 red bell pepper, cut into matchsticks
1/4 cucumber, cut into matchsticks
1/4 cup roasted salted peanuts, roughly chopped
1 cup fresh herbs (basil, mint, and/or cilantro), roughly chopped
Dipping sauce of your choice

DIRECTIONS

Fill a pie pan with very warm water. Place one wrapper in the water for 5 to 10 seconds to soften. Remove carefully and lay out on a plastic cutting board. On the lower third of the wrapper, place a small handful of the rice noodles, 2 tablespoons of the pork, and a sprinkling of the mixed vegetable matchsticks and chopped peanuts and herbs. Fold in each side of the wrapper, then roll it up tightly from the bottom like a burrito. Place seam side down, and repeat the steps above with remaining ingredients. Slice in half crosswise before serving with your favorite dipping sauce.

CHAPTER 19

At the salon, Jean found Katrin sweeping up hair while Micah and Axel danced back and forth, dueling with a pair of giant hairbrushes. They were back in their *Founders' Story* roles.

"I'll whip ye, ye scurvy ursine!" Micah cried.

"Rrrr!" Axel roared.

"Hey, Jeannie's here!" Micah dropped his hairbrush onto the floor, and so did Axel.

Katrin groaned. "Back into the sterilizer." She made a move to collect the brushes. "Oh, Isara, hi! Jean didn't tell me she was bringing a guest."

"I hope it's okay," Isara said. "I'd like to fight the thistle-berry plant. Also, I brought snacks."

"Snacks!" The boys lunged for the box.

"I'm sorry," Jean said, frowning at Micah. "It's not like they didn't both *just* have dinner."

Isara laughed. "Hey, food is made to be eaten." There was no table, so he lowered the box to a clean section of the floor and began to set things out.

"My parents prepared these appetizers before the hibernation," he said. "These are summer rolls with shredded pork. And these are crab dumplings, though they taste better warm."

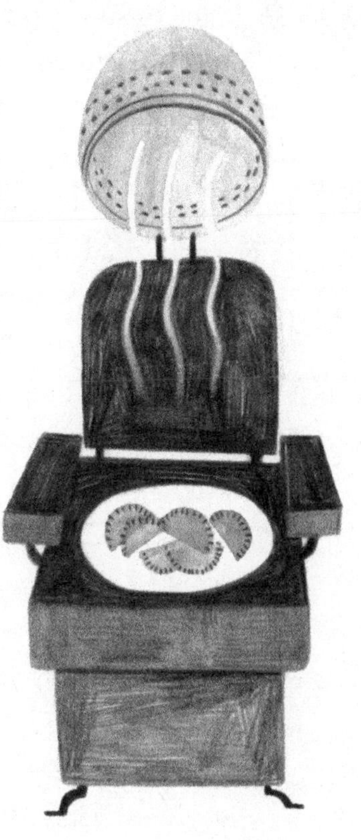

"Warm? No problem." Katrin grabbed the dumplings and popped them under a helmet-shaped hair dryer. With the flick of a switch, the machine blasted hot air down onto the food.

"Hey, Rambo, get away from there!" Micah dragged the sheep away from the summer rolls just in time.

"Let's get started," Katrin said. They all sat on the floor near the rolls. "We're meeting tonight to brainstorm how best to campaign against the construction of a thistleberry processing plant in St. Polonius. Jean, why don't you share the scientific info that you found so everyone here knows what's going on?"

"Right," Jean said. She cleared her throat and pulled Dr. Fields's flyer out of her backpack. "So, when I was at town hall the other day, I ended up in the room where they're keeping the sleepers. I found this in Dr. Fields's pocket."

Jean read the note, pausing several times so Katrin could help define the more complicated words. When she finished, Isara's brow was furrowed and the two younger boys' mouths hung wide open.

"Thistleberries are poisonous?" Micah squeaked. "But we eat them all the time!"

Katrin patted him on the arm. "Don't worry, buddy. The flyer says they're fine in small doses, like what you'd have in tea or relish. Your body can process that amount easily—that's what your liver is for. But Dr. Fields thinks that working with them in a factory, and being exposed to the toxins all day, every day, could be dangerous."

"So why didn't she tell anyone about her discovery?" Axel asked.

"We think she was about to," Katrin said, "but then the great hibernation happened before she got a chance. Right, Jean?"

But Jean didn't answer—her brain was stuck on something Katrin had just said. "What was that about liver?" she asked.

"Hm?"

"Liver," Jean repeated. "You said something about poisons and our livers."

"Oh, that," Katrin said. "It's something I know about because hair dyes, in large amounts, can be toxic, too. The liver's job is to filter your blood and suck out any poisons or other nasty things that have gotten into your body. It stores them up and processes them. But it has a limit on how much it can handle at once, which is why you don't want to expose yourself to too much in a short period."

Something was coming together for Jean. "But if the liver's job is to store up poisons—"

"Jean." Isara was holding the flyer. "Did you read this part?"

Jean leaned over to look at what he was pointing to. There was a tiny line of text at the very bottom of the page that she hadn't noticed before.

"What does it say?" Micah asked.

"It says 'CC: Mayor Theobald King,'" Isara answered. "And it has a date: October first."

"CC?" Axel asked. "What does that mean?"

"'Carbon copy,'" Isara said. "I saw that when I helped my parents with the paperwork for our restaurant. It means that a copy of this document has been sent to someone else—in this case, Mayor King."

"And it was sent on October first," Jean said. "Two whole weeks ago. So the mayor *knew* all about the dangers of opening a thistleberry plant before Founders' Day—"

"Before he made his speech encouraging our parents to vote yes!" Katrin cried.

"Dr. Fields probably thought he would tell everyone about the side effects in his speech," Jean mused. "Maybe he even told her he would. But he kept it a secret on purpose." Jean's hands balled up into fists as she remembered the "serious conversation" her parents had been having in the truck on Founders' Day. "My dad said that the mayor had already invested a bunch of the King family fortune in the plant. This is about money—he would have let our parents all get sick from working there just to keep from losing his money!"

"Whoa," Axel said.

"Okay." Micah was bouncing up and down on his heels. "So Dr. Fields didn't get to tell the town about her discovery—but we still can, right? What's the best way? Because right now, a lot of the kids are pretty excited to vote yes next week."

The group sat, thinking. Rambo waddled over and laid his head in Micah's lap.

"It smells like the crab dumplings are ready," Isara said finally. "Maybe they'll help fuel our brains."

"All right, so," Katrin said a few moments later through a mouthful of dumpling, "Jean was going to see if Dr. Fields had more flyers in her lab that we could hand out, or other information that would be useful to us. But now that lab is being guarded by B&B."

"Maybe we can make posters," Axel said. "The way the day-care kids did?"

"Yeah, but wherever we hang them, Magnus'll make

sure they get ripped down before anyone sees them," Micah said. "He's got spies everywhere now! He's probably even got them booking haircuts here, Katrin."

Katrin swallowed. "One of the kids today *did* seem eager to know how I'd be voting in the election."

"What did you say?" Jean asked.

Katrin grinned. "I told her that the more distracted I got with chatter, the more likely she was to end up with a boring haircut. That shut her up."

Axel ran a hand over his own wild hairdo. "So, uh . . . how do we know Magnus hasn't sent a spy to this meeting tonight?" He didn't say anything else, but he was looking right at Isara.

"Hey," Jean snapped. "No one in this room is a spy, okay? I *asked* Isara to come tonight. He didn't manipulate his way in or anything."

"Oh, yeah?" Axel said. "Then why isn't he eating any of the food he brought?" He turned to Isara. "No offense, dude, but that seems kind of suspicious."

Jean glanced over. Isara's plate was still empty.

"I'm not hungry," Isara said.

But Jean knew that this couldn't be true. He'd been working all night, and she hadn't seen him eat dinner. Just then, his stomach rumbled loudly, and his face flushed with embarrassment.

A half-eaten summer roll dropped to Katrin's plate. "You're lying to us," she said. "Why are you lying?"

"I'm not lying," Isara said. "I'm just not hungry for crab,

or pork. I'm never hungry for these things because . . . well, I don't like them."

"Okay, then try that goose pad thai you packed for Jean," Axel said. "You know, to prove to us that it's safe, and that you haven't been sent here by Magnus to assassinate us with snacks."

"Assassinate?" Isara shook his head. "No, please. You have this all wrong."

Jean knew Isara couldn't be trying to hurt them. He'd never do that! Okay, he wasn't eating the food tonight, but he often didn't eat the food he made for the town . . . and everyone else who'd eaten it was fine.

"Guys—" she started. Isara scrambled to his feet.

"Bar the door!" Katrin cried, and Axel took off across the room.

But Isara stood still, quaking slightly and gazing around. In the salon's mirrors, countless Isaras bounced back at him.

"I can't eat this food," he said, "because I made an oath."

"An oath to Magnus!" Axel shouted from the door. "A promise to kill us all!"

Isara shook his head. "To myself, and to the earth. I made it when I was five years old."

They all stared at him, and he took a deep breath.

"I'm not a poisoner, or a spy," he said. "I'm a vegetarian."

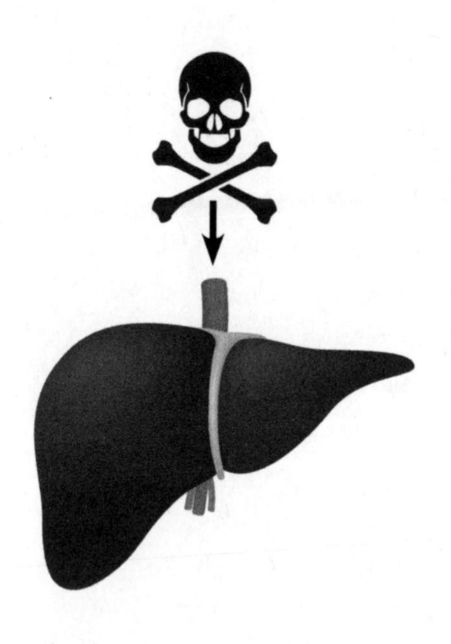

CHAPTER 20

Micah stared at Isara. “You don’t eat meat?”

“No meat, no fish, no animals,” Isara said. “When I was a small boy in Thailand, my grandfather took me fishing once. Until that day, I hadn’t realized that the fish we ate at home came from the same animals I swam with in the sea. My grandfather reeled in a large bass and clubbed it to death with a brick on the floor of the boat. There was blood everywhere.” He shuddered. “I haven’t eaten animal flesh since then.”

"But you cook it for us all the time!" Katrin cried.

"I can't avoid that," Isara said. "It's easier to get lamb and goose and fish here in St. Polonius than it is to get a lot of the vegetables I know from Thailand. My parents and I have to cook what's available for the people who want it. But that doesn't mean I have to eat it."

Axel took a tentative step away from the door. "Jean, you work with him every day," he said. "Is he telling the truth?"

Jean thought back to the meals she had seen Isara eat. Pork omelets, no. Plain rice, yes. Seafood soup, no. The cheese and jam sandwich she'd made the other night, yes (and he had even liked it).

"I think he *is* telling the truth," she said, "except for one thing." She turned to Isara. "On Founders' Day, in the tent. You *didn't* eat the liver."

Isara's ears flushed pink. "No. I didn't."

"But you pretended you had," Jean went on. "At the meeting at the schoolhouse, you specifically told Magnus you *had* eaten it. And when I asked you . . ."

He sighed. "My parents warned me not to tell anyone the truth. I think they worried that others would judge us. We may not have lived here long, but respecting traditions is important to my family—even if they're not our own." He paused, looking down at his feet. "It hasn't been easy for us, fitting in in St. Polonius. But when my parents were invited to taste the Sacred Bear Liver, they felt like we'd finally been accepted. We sat together at the play, and they made sure everyone saw me receive my portion. I pretended to eat it, but afterwards I threw it into the fjord.

"When all the adults and teenagers fell asleep," he continued, "I thought maybe it was from the liver. But then I saw you at the schoolhouse, Jean, and I knew that couldn't be the case, since you had eaten it, and you were still awake."

"But I *didn't* eat it!" Jean blurted. "Or, at least, I didn't keep it down for more than a few seconds. I got sick right outside of the tent, and threw it all up."

Micah and Katrin stared at her, and blood rushed up into her face. At long last, her terrible secret was out. "I'm sorry," she murmured to them. "I won't blame you if you're ashamed of me."

But Micah jumped up and grabbed her hand. "It's okay," he whispered. Tears of gratitude pricked Jean's eyes.

Katrin stood up, too, and Jean braced herself. "You really didn't eat it?" Katrin said. "Why didn't you tell us sooner?"

Jean's voice quavered. "I didn't tell anyone. Well, my parents knew. They saw me get sick. But they said I shouldn't let word get out—like Isara's parents did, I guess. And I understand why: Magnus suspects me, and that day he called me into his office, he kept talking about how he'd have to enforce the law and punish me if he turned up any evidence. . . ."

Jean trailed off. Would Katrin agree with Magnus, that Jean needed to be punished? She was Jean's best friend—but her faith was important to her, too. If she thought that the hibernation was a result of Jean's mistake, she might just be the witness that Magnus was looking for.

Finally, Katrin spoke. "Then this all means . . . that the hibernation *could* have been caused by that bad liver! Jean, you were right all along!"

Jean's mouth fell open.

"What?" Katrin asked.

"I guess," Jean started, "I guess I thought . . . you know, since you and your mom go to church . . ."

Katrin sighed. "Jean, believing in the saints doesn't mean that I don't *also* believe in science—especially when the evidence is sitting right in front of me. Plus, I doubt the saints would have wanted *anyone* to eat liver that was toxic. They wouldn't want to see you punished; if anything, they'd be glad you threw yours up!"

Jean couldn't keep a grin from breaking across her face. She had admitted her greatest failing in life, and her best friend seemed to think she'd done something good!

Only Axel still frowned. "Wait," he said. "What do you mean *toxic* liver? My dad and I butchered that bear ourselves—I know that the liver we delivered to the mayor was fresh!"

"I believe you," Jean said. "But I don't think that *that* liver is the one that ended up getting served on Founders' Day."

"What?"

Jean and Isara quickly filled him in about their discovery of two different bags of liver in Mr. Miller's freezer of horrors. Axel shook his head. "That doesn't make any sense," he said. "Every good hunter in the North Country knows not to hunt for bears at high altitude—they're hard to find up there. We found ours on the slopes outside of town, at a lower elevation. Where could the other one have come from?"

"Maybe Mr. Miller knew somebody," Jean said. "He

must have had shady connections who got him those shark fins and whale meat."

"Or maybe," Axel said, "he hunted it himself, for sport. My dad's always said that Burt Miller was a total weirdo, but a pretty good shot."

"Well, however it happened, it looks like everyone ate the high-altitude bear liver," Jean said, "which I guess is toxic somehow? Katrin says all livers store toxins in them."

"True," Katrin said. "So maybe bears that live at higher altitudes eat more toxic stuff than bears that live at lower ones." She turned to Axel. "What do you think, bear expert?"

Axel scratched his nearly bald head. "That could be," he said. "There's less food for bears at the highest altitudes—more different kinds of plants and animals live a little lower. That's why most hunters stick to tracking there. The higher up you go, the less chance you have of finding a bear, because it's harder for *them* to find food up there."

"So what kind of food would a high-altitude bear eat?" Micah asked.

"Well," Axel said, "the higher you go, the smaller the plants get. Once you're above the tree line, all that's left are grasses and shrubs. So they'd eat whatever grows on shrubs. Like . . ."

"Like thistleberries," Jean said.

The room hushed, and Jean knelt to pick up Dr. Fields's flyer. The pieces of the puzzle were finally clicking together, and she needed to talk the whole thing out before her brain lost its grip on the picture it was forming.

"So a bear living at high altitude ate a bunch of thistleberries," she started. "Its liver filtered out the poison and stored it up, but before it could process everything, someone—probably Mr. Miller—came along and killed it. When its liver got served to the people of St. Polonius, they each got a mega-dose of thistleberry toxin . . . and fell into a coma."

Katrin looked livid. "And all because some squid-brain mixed up the two bags?"

Jean held out the flyer. "I don't think there *was* a mix-up. Think about it: Dr. Fields showed Mayor King how poisonous thistleberries could be at high concentrations, thinking he would use that information for the good of the town. But he was committed to building a plant to process thistleberries by then—and he *knew* that if this news got out, the project would be sunk." Jean stumbled on, feeling the puzzle pieces snap into place as she went. "But . . . then . . . someone *also* must have realized that if they could feed all the adults in town a high concentration of thistleberries, then they might fall asleep for a long time. If they did, their kids would have to vote in their places . . . and Magnus could convince the kids to pass the proposal that their parents would never vote through!"

She stopped there, slightly out of breath. The others were looking at her like she'd just spouted one of Mr. Miller's own wackadoodle conspiracy theories.

"Jean," Axel said finally, "I know you don't like Magnus. But he's the biggest rule-follower I've ever met! Do you honestly think he and his dad *purposely* put the whole town to sleep, using bear liver they knew was toxic, so they could steal a vote in the election?"

"Actually," Jean said, "I'm not sure Magnus's father was involved. I saw him and his wife asleep in that room in town hall, alongside everyone else. Do you think he would poison himself?" She shook her head. "I think Magnus switched the livers on his own. We know he knew about them—remember the meeting at the schoolhouse? He said he'd gone along with his dad when the livers were inspected by Dr. Fields. He knew exactly which one was safe and which one wasn't, and what would happen if everyone ate the toxic one."

Jean didn't blame the other kids for staring at her in astonishment. Finally, Katrin cleared her throat. "Not to change the subject," she said, "but does anyone remember, in *The Founders' Story,* what the narrator said right before the bear walked into the sailors' camp?"

Jean glanced at her brother, who she knew had pretty much memorized the play backward and forward. She nodded at him, and he cleared his throat. "I do. He says, 'But then, one day, when all seemed lost, a bear staggered down from the high mountains and into the camp. Captain Polonius bravely drew his cutlass—' "

"That's it," Katrin said. "So the story says the bear came from the high mountains. And that it staggered—so it had trouble walking, right?"

The others nodded.

"Couldn't that be because its liver was already full of thistleberry toxin, and the poison was making it sleepy?"

Jean stared at her. "That's brilliant," she said. "If that's true, then maybe even the *original* great hibernation was caused by thistleberry poison!"

"I'm not sure we should take the wording so seriously, guys," Axel said. "It's just an old legend."

But Dad had told them: even the tallest tales can hold a grain of truth.

Micah, at least, seemed to be changing his mind. "This is wild," he said. "A high-altitude bear right there in *The Founders' Story*!"

"Yeah," Isara chimed in. "Well thought out, Katrin."

"Thanks," she said. "We study the old stories a lot at church." She cleared her throat then. "And, Isara, I'm sorry that we accused you of, you know . . . being a spy, and all that. It was really stupid. Right, Axel?" She gave the boy a hard shove.

"Right," Axel said. "Sorry, Isara."

Isara nodded. "I appreciate your apology. But now what will we do with all this new information?"

"Right!" Katrin said to the group. "What can we do? We still have to wait for the poison to wear off, and for the adults to wake up, before we can talk to Dr. Fields and confirm everything. Meanwhile, the other kids are all set to vote for the thistleberry plant on Saturday."

"Yeah," Axel added, "and if Magnus was willing to poison the whole town to win a vote, who knows what he might do to *us* if he finds out we're working against him? Especially now that he's got spies everywhere. Spreading the word about Dr. Fields's discovery—even on the sly—could be dangerous."

They stood in silence. Jean glanced down at the flyer. "It says here that Dr. Fields was 'working to formulate an antidote' to the thistleberry poison. A cure. I wonder how far she got."

"Her notes are probably locked up in her lab, so that's not helpful to us," Katrin said.

"True," said Micah. "But if we *could* get into her office, and we *could* find her notes, maybe we could mix up a batch of the cure! And if we cured all the grown-ups before Saturday . . ."

"Then they'd be able to vote in the election!" Jean finished. "And with Dr. Fields awake to tell everyone about the mayor's big cover-up, there's no way anyone would still want to vote in favor of the plant."

"I agree," Isara said. "So what's blocking access to the lab?"

"One locked door," Jean answered, "and two Smuthers twins."

"They're basically living in the hallway," Micah explained. "They're there when I get in to my dad's office in the morning, and they stay after everyone's left for the night. Magnus sends someone to bring them their meals from the restaurant. I think he's paying them a bunch of money out of the town treasury—I heard them talking about it."

"Is there another way we could bust in?" Katrin asked. "Through a window?"

"If they're anything like the windows in my dad's office," Micah said, "they're triple glazed and bolted shut. Built for insulation—though they're not doing much good with the heating system still brok—"

He froze midword, his eyes bulging slightly. "That's it!" he whispered.

"Micah?" Jean asked.

"The heating system!" he breathed. "It's still broken!"

"Okaaay," Katrin said. "But what does that have to do with our situation?"

"The little bit of heat we do get comes into the office through vents," Micah explained. "I know where my dad's is, because Rambo likes to curl up next to it. It's down in the corner on one of the walls he shares with Dr. Fields's office. That means there must be a vent into her office in that wall, too!"

"Whoa," Axel said. "So there *is* another way in!"

"Exactly!" Micah cried. "So if I can take off the grating in Dad's office, then I should be able to crawl through the heating ducts—"

"Wait a second," Jean interrupted. "Crawl through the heating ducts? That sounds dangerous. Isn't the whole system on the fritz?"

"It's only working at half capacity," Micah said, "but actually, that's great. If it was on full throttle, then the ducts would be too hot to crawl through. Since they're only half heated, it should be fine!"

"*Half* heated? *Should* be fine?" Jean didn't like the sound of this. Only a few short days ago, she'd thought Micah might be lost to frostbite. "There must be another way in. Or . . . or I can do it."

Micah shook his head. "The vent's small, Jeannie. I don't think anyone else here could fit into it, except maybe for Axel. But what excuse would he have to come into my office? I'm already there every day. It makes more sense for me to go."

"No!" Jean looked around at the others pleadingly, but no one said anything. Micah wasn't *their* brother—he wasn't the one person they had sworn to protect during this hibernation.

"You can't stop me, Jeannie," Micah said quietly. "This may be our only chance to prevent the thistleberry plant from getting built—*and* to show Magnus and his dad that they can't just do whatever they want and get away with it. Who knows how long everyone might stay in this hibernation otherwise?"

Jean knew he had a point, though that didn't make her feel any better about his plan. "I won't stop you," she said, "but I want to be there when you go in. B&B know I visit you at work sometimes, so it shouldn't be too weird for me to show up in the middle of the day. And that way, if *anything* goes wrong, at least you'll have help."

"Good idea," Katrin said, and Isara and Axel nodded.

"Okay, come see me tomorrow afternoon," Micah said. "Sometimes after lunch, at least one of the Bs nods off for a while. With a little luck, we'll have the cure by dinner!"

Katrin grinned. "Let's all meet back here tomorrow night, then, to do some chemistry."

"Yeah," Isara added. "And if there are any ingredients from my kitchen that'll help make the antidote, Jean and I can bring them. And snacks!"

The kids cleared their plates and Isara and Axel headed home, excited about the plan. But Jean knew she would hardly sleep a wink. Not since the night before the spelling bee had she gone to bed so nervous about what the next day might bring.

Plan for Operation
Wakey-Wakey

Scriven'd by the hand of
Katrin Ash

Micah: Crawl into Dr. Fields's office to retrieve antidote formula

Jean: Provide cover for Micah in case of emergency

Katrin: Amass materials at Ash Beauty 'n Tattoo for chemistry project

Isara: Provide helpful ingredients from pantry (and snacks)

Axel: keep roads clear as usual

CHAPTER 21

I'm just here for a visit.

Jean practiced saying this in her head as she walked toward the university building the next afternoon.

A regular old visit with my brother, nothing strange about that.

She tried to breathe deeply, but the bitter cold stung her nose and throat. Even the air seemed out to get her.

Katrin had offered to cancel her afternoon hair appointments to go with Jean to Micah's office, and Axel had volunteered to drive them both in the snowplow. But Jean didn't want anything to look out of the ordinary to Magnus's spies. She and Micah had to pull this off alone.

Inside the university building, Bartleby and Bertha loomed larger with every step she took. They had littered the floor around their feet with paper cups, and their mouths were stained brown with cocoa.

"Good afternoon, Waitress Huddy!" Bartleby's voice was somewhere between a bark and a burp.

"I'mjusthereforavisit!" The words came out of Jean's mouth both faster and squeakier than she'd intended. She ducked into Micah's office and shut the door tightly before B&B could respond.

"You're here!" Micah jumped up from their dad's rolling chair. "Wanna help me move Rambo out of his favorite spot?"

They spent the next five minutes trying to coax the sheep away from the vent in the corner, which was blowing the mildest of warm breezes into the room. Finally, remembering Rambo's fondness for things he shouldn't eat, Jean retrieved their dad's bonsai pine from its spot high on the windowsill. Shaking its needles in Rambo's face, she lured him across the room.

"Thanks!" Micah said, and crouched by the vent. In seconds, he had pried the grate off and strapped a headlamp to his forehead.

"We don't want people to hear anything, so I can't call back to you through the vent," Micah reminded her.

"I know," Jean said. "Just get back here as fast as you can, okay? If you find the formula, great, but the most important thing is that you stay safe."

"And don't get caught."

Jean swallowed. She didn't even want to think about what B&B would do if Micah fell into their clutches.

She wanted to spring forward and hug him, but was afraid Rambo might go nuts if she let go of his scarf-leash. So she gave Micah what she hoped was a breezy, encouraging wave. "Good luck!"

Micah waved back, then crouched down. A moment later, like an arctic lamprey wriggling into a sea cave, he was in the wall.

Jean watched the second hand tick by on Dad's wall clock for three interminable minutes, then finally released her grip on the fidgety Rambo. The sheep must have absorbed some of her anxiety; once freed, he paced, letting out a series of whimpery *baaahs*. "You and me both, boy." Jean began to pace, too.

After six minutes, Jean was wishing she and Micah had made a plan: *If you're gone for more than ten minutes, I'll squeeze in after you*—something like that. Jean thought of her parents, still sound asleep on the farmhouse floor. If something happened to Micah on her watch, would they ever forgive her? Would she ever forgive herself?

A sudden noise made her heart freeze. Only a creak, but a familiar one: the sound of Dr. Fields's ancient file cabinet opening. It was half rusted, and Jean had once been nearly deafened by it while helping file papers. "We've been requesting new furniture from the main campus for years," Dr. Fields had said.

Why, oh why, hadn't Jean warned Micah about the drawers?

Another creak, louder. Jean began to panic. If she could hear it in her dad's office, then surely the Smuthers twins heard it in the hallway! Cracking the office door open a tiny bit, she peeked out. Bertha and a drowsy-looking Bartleby were on their feet.

"Did you hear that?" Bartleby asked his sister, yawning.

"Of course I did! Give me the key to the lab."

"What key?"

"The one we took out of that scientist's pocket at town hall!"

"Oh, right." Bartleby patted his police vest.

Without thinking, Jean barged out into the hallway. "Hey, guys!" she called, waving.

"What do you want?" Bartleby asked, digging into a pocket.

A third creak. Louder.

"I WANTED TO KNOW," Jean bellowed, "if you have any special requests from the restaurant. You know, for MEALS or SNACKS! Isara and I like to support law enforcement any way we can!"

She was just making things up now, but it seemed to work. Bartleby paused in his key search. "I'd love some more of those crispy bananas. Can Isara send an order over?"

Bertha cuffed him on the side of his head. "Shut up and get me that key!"

"Right." Bartleby plunged his hand into another pocket and felt around. "Wait—I didn't put it in my pocket. It's in my shoe!" He yanked off his boot.

Jean lunged for the boot—and a blinding pain shot through her right knee. Time seemed to slow as her leg gave way under her, and it wasn't until she was on the floor looking up that she saw the nightstick in Bertha's hand.

"You hit me!" Jean cried.

"Request for backup at the university building!" Bertha shouted into a walkie-talkie. "Request for backup! Police under attack!"

"I didn't attack you!"

"Perpetrator caught in the act of lunging for an officer's weapon!"

"Oh, come on," Jean protested. "A boot is not a weapon!"

"Oh, yeah?" Bertha snapped the walkie-talkie back onto her belt. "Tell that to *my* boot while it breaks all your fingers!"

She lifted her foot right over Jean's hand. Jean snatched it out of the way as Bertha's heavy sole stomped onto the hallway floor.

She's insane! Jean thought. She tried to push herself back up to her feet, but her right knee throbbed painfully beneath her. All she could do was scuttle down the hallway like a crab.

Bertha growled, "Let's get 'er, brother."

At least, Jean thought, *I'm drawing them away from the lab door.* By the time B&B were done busting up the rest of her limbs, Micah would have had the chance to crawl back to Dad's office . . . hopefully with the secret formula.

Jean's head smacked painfully into two walls; she had literally backed herself into a corner. B&B raised their nightsticks high, and Jean feebly lifted her arms to shield her head from the oncoming blows.

"STOP!"

The twins whirled around. The door to Dr. Fields's lab had flown open, and Micah came charging out. "GET AWAY FROM MY SISTER!"

"Micah, no!" Jean groaned. Too late.

"It was *you* inside that office!" Bertha cried. "Breaking and entering!"

Micah was at least a head shorter than the twins, but he barreled forward with the force of a cannonball. "Lay another finger on my sister," he snarled, "and I'll break and enter your *face.*"

Bartleby's boot clunked from his hand to the floor. "Hey!" he cried. "You'd better watch your mouth when you're talking to *my* sister!"

Micah ignored him and dropped down beside Jean. "Are you okay?"

A mighty draft shot through the hallway as the building's main door banged open, and the floor under Jean began to shake with the pounding of footsteps.

"I'll be fine," she insisted, lowering her voice. "Did you get it?"

Micah nodded. "It's simple. We just have to feed them a solution that's—"

A gloved hand clapped over Micah's mouth, and two sets of arms dragged him backward.

Micah flailed. "Don't hurt him!" Jean screamed. Liddy Dowell and Kris Thornhill, both with police badges pinned to their chests, were holding her brother while the twins circled them. Terrified of what they might do, she cried, "Micah, don't struggle!"

He listened. His arms flopped like two dead fish as Bertha pulled a length of rope out of her vest and bound his wrists behind him. All the while, a gloved hand remained over Micah's mouth—a hand that belonged to the interim mayor himself.

"Micah Huddy," Magnus intoned, "as mayor of St. Polonius-on-the-Fjord, I am charged with maintaining law and order. For the good of the town, I am placing you under arrest.

"You are required to remain silent," he continued, though that didn't sound right to Jean. Still, the less the mayor and his cronies learned about what Micah had been up to, the better. Gently, almost imperceptibly, Jean shook her head. Micah blinked, which Jean took to mean that he understood.

"Deputy Constable Bartleby," Magnus said, "please lock the lab door. Constable Bertha and other officers, take Micah Huddy down to the police station for booking."

"Hang on!" Using her good leg and the wall for leverage, Jean pushed herself to her feet. She held out her wrists.

"Got another piece of rope for me?" If Micah was being taken to the station, she was going right along with him.

Magnus raised a blond eyebrow. "What for?"

"To arrest me with," Jean said. "For attacking an officer. Tell him, Bertha."

Bertha glanced at Magnus. To Jean's surprise, Magnus gave Bertha the exact same subtle head shake she had just given Micah.

And, like Micah, Bertha got it. "I have no idea what she's talking about. Her brother's the only one we saw committing a crime."

"Then off to jail with him," Magnus said, "and him alone. Ms. Huddy, you may return to your place of employment."

"Now, just a minute—" Jean started, but Magnus and the others had already turned toward the exit. Liddy and Kris had their arms linked with her brother's so they could frog-march him out of the building.

Magnus could easily have arrested Jean. He was separating her from her brother on purpose.

"Wait—Micah—no!" Jean lurched forward, but her knee faltered. She slid to the ground, cursing Bertha and her nightstick.

She heard a loud *baaah* and turned to see Rambo's muzzle poking out of the doorway of Dad's office. At the sound, Micah's head twisted back over his shoulder, and his gaze caught Jean's.

Take care of my sheep? his brown eyes seemed to ask.

Her own eyes, filling with tears, promised: *I will.*

Arrest record for:
Micah Huddy
Date:
Thursday, October 19
Location:
Great Northern University–
St. Polonius-on-the-Fjord Extension
Charges:
Breaking, entering, and more to
be determined
By the order of:
Magnus King
Interim Mayor & Magistrate

CHAPTER 22

The building's door slammed shut. Jean was alone.

Pushing herself up once more on her good leg, she hopped toward Dad's office door. Rambo let her lean on his strong back. "Good sheep," she murmured as they hobbled to the desk.

Her hands shook as she dialed the salon's number; the phone lines in town, unlike the one out to the farm, were still intact.

Katrin picked up. "Ash Beauty and Tattoo! How can I make you look awesome today?"

"Micah's been arrested," Jean rasped.

"What? Hang on." The sound from the phone grew muffled, but Jean could hear Katrin telling her current client to get lost. Then, "Jean! What happened?"

Jean was about to tell her everything when an awful thought occurred to her: What if Magnus had a spy working the local telephone switchboard? Whatever she said might be listened to, or even recorded.

"Look," she said, "it's a long story, and my knee is hurt, so . . . do you think you could track Axel down and come over in his snowplow to pick me up? They've taken Micah to the police station, but I don't think I can walk all that way without help."

"Of course," Katrin said. "Sit tight—I'll gather the gang. And oh, Jean . . . I'm sorry."

Twenty minutes later, Katrin and Isara burst through Dad's office door.

"We're here!" Katrin gasped. "Axel's parking. But, Jean—"

She didn't have a chance to finish her sentence. "Out of our way!" little Annemarie Hammerstein cried. "Emergency medical professionals coming through!"

Wearing a white coat that dragged on the floor and carrying a big black medical bag, the doctor's daughter shoved Jean's friends aside and barreled into the room. Lars Ludavisk followed close on her heels, a superhero cape draped over his dad's too-big medic uniform.

Jean shot Katrin a furious look. "You brought *them*?"

"It's not her fault," Isara said as he gathered up Rambo's scarf-leash. "They were at the Tasty Thai Hut when she came for me, and when they heard her say you'd hurt your knee, they insisted on coming."

"It's my duty as a doctor to help the injured and infirm," Annemarie announced proudly. "My stitching's really good—I've been practicing on my dollies all week!" She pulled a doll out of the medical bag to show them all. Its rag limbs had been severed and reattached—to its head.

Isara's eyes widened, and Katrin's purple-painted lips froze into a round O.

The stitching *was* very neat, though.

"Nice work," Jean said, trying to act casual, "but I don't need any stitches. I just need to go find my brother." She pushed herself up out of the office chair, but when she took a step her knee collapsed under her weight.

Annemarie swooped in. "Hold still while I examine you. I know how to take care of knees. Lars, my reflex hammer, please." Lars reached into the bag and produced what looked like a triangle on a stick.

"Does it hurt when I do this?" Annemarie whacked the hammer against Jean's knee in the exact same spot Bertha had struck. Jean howled.

"Yup." Annemarie tossed the hammer aside. "It'll have to come off."

Jean choked. *"What?"*

"No time to lose! Lars, clear this surface for operation. And get my scalpel!"

Lars swept all Jean's dad's papers and books off his desk and onto the floor, then pulled the scalpel out of the black bag. "Got it!"

The office door flew open again, and Jean had never been so glad to see Axel Gorson in her life. His gray eyes darted back and forth. "Whoa," he said. "What's going on?"

Everyone started shouting at once—everyone but Jean, who shot Axel a look that said "Get us out of here!"

"Roger that," Axel said, and in a twirling leap reminiscent of his bear dance in *The Founders' Story,* he vaulted past Lars and over the desk to land behind Jean. He rammed the

back of her rolling chair, sending it flying around the side of the desk. Annemarie and Lars jumped aside. The scalpel fell to the floor, and Isara toed it out of the way with a perfectly executed soccer kick.

"Let's go!" Axel cried. They dashed into the hallway, Axel pushing Jean, Katrin and Isara pulling Rambo. They shot past Bartleby, who was guarding Dr. Fields's door, and didn't stop until they were piled into the snowplow's cab.

"Police brutality!" Katrin cried once Jean had finished telling them how she'd been injured. "Bertha can't just go around kneecapping people. There are laws about this kind of thing!"

"Yeah!" Axel said, jamming his sled-slab a little too hard into the gas pedal.

"Don't worry, I'll heal," Jean said. "Micah's the one who needs our help." She summarized Micah's arrest as fast as she could. "So I guess if there's any good news," she concluded, "it's that he said he found a formula. But he didn't have time to tell me before they hauled him away."

"That's *great* news!" Isara said. "So when we get him out of jail, we'll be able to start waking people up!"

"But how are we going to get him out?" Jean asked.

"I've got a plan—follow my lead," Katrin said as the truck jolted to a stop in front of the station.

Axel shoved the gearshift into park. "All riiiight!" he cried. "Let's go bust someone outta lockup!"

Leaving Rambo in the cab, Katrin and Isara helped Jean down the snowy sidewalk. With every halting step,

Jean thought of Mom. How would she handle this situation? She'd be calm, but forceful; she'd know her rights; she wouldn't let Magnus and his cronies intimidate her.

Jean took a deep breath and pushed open the station door.

Inside, the building was small but bright, fluorescent lights illuminating the desks that normally belonged to Constable Elaine Smuthers and her deputy, Peter MacNish. Deputy MacNish didn't have children, though Jean remembered from her class trip to the station that he collected cheerful little animal figurines—yellow dogs, pink pussycats—and kept them on his desk. But they weren't there now; B&B must have removed them.

Bertha sat behind her mother's desk, and Magnus, Liddy, and Kris were hanging around the station's water cooler. Next to that cooler was the thick door that led to the jail cell in back.

Bertha jumped to her feet. "What are *you* all doing here?"

"We're here for Micah Huddy," Axel said.

Bertha's hands moved to her hips. "He's been arrested, so he's not allowed to leave. Unless you can afford his bail, which seems unlikely."

"Try us." Katrin stepped forward and pulled a thick wad of cash out of her coat pocket. Jean's heart lurched—it was her earnings from the salon, the money Katrin was saving for the Inkmaster 3000.

"How much is it?" Katrin asked.

Magnus strode forward, smiling like he was welcoming them to a tea party. "Greetings, Ms. Ash," he said. "To answer your question, bail hasn't been set yet. Judge Barrett's only daughter is sixteen, so she's in hibernation along with her parents. Luckily, the town charter has a clause that covers this type of situation." He motioned to Liddy, who scurried over with a thick binder; apparently, Magnus now carried a copy of the charter everywhere he went.

"Article 312, clause 17," he read. *"In the case of incapacitation of the local magistrate*—spelled *M-A-G-I-S-T-R-A-T-E,* that's a fancy word for judge—*the town's highest-ranking elected official shall oversee all legal proceedings."*

"The town's highest-ranking elected official?" Jean couldn't help but sputter. "But that would be . . ."

"Yes," Magnus said, stroking his spelling-bee medal. "That would be me."

He locked eyes with Jean. "Therefore," he continued, "in my first official decision as acting local magistrate, I set Micah Huddy's bail at . . ." He grabbed a piece of scrap paper from the deputy's desk and scribbled down a number.

A number, followed by *five* zeroes.

Jean's hurt knee buckled, and Isara's arm squeezed her in support.

Axel, meanwhile, looked ready to punch someone. "Magnus," he growled, "that's *crazy.*"

"That's Mr. Mayor, if you please."

Katrin grabbed Axel's arm, holding him back before he could do anything stupid. "Come on, *Mr. Mayor,*" she said, fanning the bills in her hand out in front of him. "I've got over three hundred right here. Surely that's a fair bail for Micah. I mean, all he did was bust into the office next door to his—he was probably looking for extra pens or something." Jean, Isara, and Axel nodded.

But Magnus snorted. "Ms. Ash, I agree that three hundred would be a fair bail if all Micah Huddy was charged with was breaking and entering. But those crimes are only the tip of the iceberg."

"What do you mean?" Jean asked.

Magnus leaned forward on the desk. "What I mean is that your brother has *also* been charged with the much more serious crimes of espionage and high treason."

"Espionage?" Isara asked.

"Yes," Magnus replied. "*Espionage: E-S-P-I-O-N-A-G-E.* It means spying. And high treason means betraying your government." He was still looking directly at Jean. "We have evidence that your Bigsbyan friend, Dr. Mary Fields, was planning to sabotage the upcoming election. And if your brother was helping her . . ."

"What?" Jean shook her head. Evidence? Magnus must have meant the flyer Dr. Fields had sent the mayor. But she was just trying to share her scientific findings. And Micah had nothing to do with that, anyway.

"We'll question Dr. Fields when she wakes up in the spring," Magnus continued. "And if she's found guilty . . . well, foreigners who aren't loyal to the St. Polonian government can always be shipped back to where they came from." He shifted his gaze to Isara as he said this, and Jean felt the boy's grip on her shoulder tighten.

"But your brother is awake, so his trial will proceed. Don't worry—he'll have a lawyer. In fact, she's on her way."

"I want to see him," Jean said. "Prisoners are allowed visitors."

"That, like bail, is for the judge to decide," Magnus said. "And I'm afraid that this prisoner is too dangerous to be allowed to speak with anyone other than his attorney."

It took every ounce of self-control Jean had not to launch herself at Magnus right there and then. Instead she hobbled around the desk, dragging Isara with her. "I'm going to see my brother," she said, "and you can't stop me."

But he could. At a wave of Magnus's hand, Bertha was on her feet and moving to block the door, her nightstick out before Jean had even made it five feet. "Watch yourself, Huddy."

Jean's fury with the girl who had hit her boiled over. "And if I don't?" she spat back. "Then you can go ahead and arrest me, too!"

"So you can conspire with your brother in jail?" Magnus asked. "No, I think not. House arrest out at your farm would be a much better option; I'm sure that Constable Smuthers would be more than happy to accompany you there."

Katrin hurried over and took Jean's hand. "Don't do anything you'll regret," she whispered into her ear. "Come—we'll figure this out."

Jean *wanted* to do something she'd regret, but Katrin was right. Getting herself exiled to the farm wasn't going to free Micah, or help wake up all the sleepers. She took a step backward. *Yowch*—her knee.

"Mr. Mayor," Isara asked, "can we at least deliver meals for the prisoner?"

"Yes, of course," Magnus said. "See, Ms. Huddy, you have nothing to worry about. Your brother will be treated well while he awaits his trial."

"And when will this trial be?" Katrin asked.

"In two days. Saturday."

"Two days?" Jean cried. On one hand, that sounded like an eternity for her little brother—who hated being cooped up—to spend in jail, alone. But on the other, it didn't sound like it gave him (and his lawyer, whoever that was) much time to prepare a defense.

"Yes, in two days," Magnus repeated. "A public trial will begin in the morning at town hall, before the vote. A seven-person jury will be selected from Micah's peers, and the lawyers will make their arguments. As the town charter states, a simple majority will convict or acquit the accused, though the final sentencing will be at the discretion of the judge . . . that is, me."

"And what kind of sentence would Micah face if he was convicted?" Jean asked.

Bertha sneered. "Don't you know anything about the penal code of St. Polonius? Throughout our history, all high crimes have had the same punishment: marooning on an ice floe."

"Marooning?" Jean knew that her voice sounded faint, but she couldn't help it. That was the very punishment she'd been fearing if the mayor learned she had thrown up her liver. But she would maroon herself a hundred times over if it meant freeing her brother.

Katrin was shocked, too. "You would leave an eight-year-old boy alone on an ice floe in the North Sea? Magnus, you *can't*."

"That's *Mr. Mayor,*" Magnus said pleasantly, "and no one is marooning anyone yet. After all, if the thistleberry plant measure passes on Saturday, I might be in such an excellent mood that I'd be willing to commute the boy's entire sentence!"

So *that* was what this was all about. Magnus suspected that Jean and her friends were working to sway the thistleberry vote. He'd locked Micah up to scare them into stopping their campaign.

A blast of cold air whipped through the room as the door to the station swung open. "Ah, here she is," Magnus said. "Counsel for the defense. How are you today, Interim Public Defender Buggins?"

Jean turned toward the door, then had to lower her gaze by about a foot. Seven-year-old Cora Buggins was standing there in a fuzzy hat and snow boots, her stuffed narwhal dangling from one hand and her attorney mother's briefcase clutched in the other.

"Hi!" she said brightly. "Where's Micah? Can I see him? My associate Spike and I are ready to do some lawyering!"

For a moment, Jean wondered whether Spike was a fellow kid lawyer. Then she realized Cora was talking about the narwhal.

"I'll take you back to see your client," Magnus said, and he escorted Cora past Jean. Bertha stepped aside to let the two through the door to the jail, and it slammed shut behind them.

“Come on, Jean,” Katrin said gently. “Let’s go make Micah a sandwich, or something.”

“Yeah,” Axel said with a grunt. “He’ll probably be starving after dealing with these clowns.”

Leaving Micah in jail was the last thing Jean wanted, but she let Katrin and Isara help her toward the exit.

As she passed the deputy’s desk, she realized that the toy animal collection wasn’t gone at all. The figurines were dangling from the underside of the desk, tape wrapped around each of their little necks like nooses.

In Justice We Trust!

~~JADE H.~~ CORA P. BUGGINS (and Spike!), ~~J.D.~~

Attorneys-at-Law

CHAPTER 23

Back in the truck's cab, everyone was silent. Finally, Axel started the engine and maneuvered the truck through the snowy streets.

When he parked around the corner from the Tasty Thai Hut, Katrin exploded. "This is so unfair!" she cried. "If Jean's theory about the liver is right, then Magnus is the biggest criminal around. What gives him the right to lock Micah up?" She kicked the truck's door with her combat boot. "Our parents would *never* let an eight-year-old boy sit in jail like that, no matter what he had done. Not even Magnus's father would be so cruel."

"Yeah," Axel said. "And the worst part is, Micah has the formula that can wake our parents up! If we'd just been able to get it from him, we could have ended this."

"Maybe we can still figure something out," Isara said. "Some way to get to Micah—or another way to break into Dr. Fields's office. Can we meet again at the salon after dinner?"

"Yes!" Katrin and Axel cried.

Jean nodded, still unable to speak. She doubted meeting would do much.

Katrin coaxed Rambo down from the cab, and Axel and Isara helped Jean. In the dining room, kids were making their own sandwiches with the jam and cheese and bread Isara had left out for them, spilling sticky jam all over the place.

"I'll get the rags," Jean mumbled, but Isara laid a hand on her arm.

"No way," he said. "You'll sit in the pantry with ice on your leg. Then we'll make food to bring Micah."

"Thanks, Isara."

Rambo wasn't allowed in the kitchen—"Health code violations," Isara protested—so Katrin kept an eye on him out front. Isara set Jean up in the pantry with her leg on a crate, then brought her a bag of ice from the freezer and one crutch. "My mother's crutch, from when she twisted her ankle a few months ago," he said. "She had two, but I can't seem to find the other one."

Jean sat still, letting her knee go numb under the ice. Her friends were taking care of her, but there was no one to take care of Micah in jail. If only she could talk to him, she would apologize—tell him that she was sorry she hadn't covered for him better, sorry she had let him down.

Ten minutes later, Isara rushed back into the pantry. "Jean—everyone out there's been talking about the arrest. And now Magnus is about to make a speech!"

She threw her ice bag to the ground. "Hand me the crutch."

He did, and they made it through the door just as Magnus was climbing up on his chair to address the room.

"Ladies and gentlemen," Magnus said, "my sources tell me that some wild rumors are circulating, and I'd like to put them to rest."

Your sources? Jean thought bitterly. *You mean your spies.*

"You may have heard that there was an arrest today in St. Polonius-on-the-Fjord. This is true. Micah Huddy is currently in jail."

Gasps echoed around the room. "Micah?" Jean heard a girl at a nearby table ask. "The boy who played Captain Polonius in the play?"

"He's so nice," another kid said.

"What did he do?" someone shouted.

Magnus cleared his throat. "Micah Huddy was apprehended breaking and entering an off-limits office at the university building. Though he may be implicated—*I-M-P-L-I-C-A-T-E-D,* which means 'closely connected'—in more serious crimes. All will be made clear at his trial on Saturday morning."

He paused, and his medal gave a near-blinding flash as it caught the restaurant's overhead light. "As you know, this town's laws will be taken seriously while I'm mayor."

Jean could barely contain her snort of laughter. All the laws—except the one against poisoning a large group of people! She would have climbed onto a chair herself and shouted out everything she suspected, if only she thought anyone would believe her.

"To prevent another such break-in," Magnus continued, "I've stationed guards not only at the university building, but also at town hall, to protect the sleepers."

A concerned murmur moved through the room. "Has someone threatened them?" Eliza Johanssen asked.

"No," Magnus said, "but I don't want anyone to worry about their sleeping family members. My forces and I will keep them safe. However, if you have any suspicions—any inkling that someone is about to act against the best interests of this town—I *urge* you to share them with me. Perhaps if someone had done so in this situation, Micah Huddy wouldn't have had a chance to commit his crimes in the first place."

So Magnus was guarding their parents now. And he wanted everyone to be a spy, whether they were wearing a police badge or not.

He climbed down from his chair, and Jean slumped against the kitchen doorframe. Everything seemed so hopeless. The kids at the nearest table were already giving their neighbors the side-eye, probably planning what they'd say when they tattled on each other to the mayor.

But down on the floor, a few kids seemed more suspicious of Magnus than of each other.

"Breaking and entering?" Jean heard Jack Perigee say in a low voice. "What do you think he was trying to steal?"

"Maybe nothing," Jillian Seidel-Mitchell replied. "Maybe the mayor just doesn't like him."

"Yeah, but that's not a reason to throw someone in jail, is it?" another kid asked.

Jillian raised an eyebrow. "I get the feeling that our new mayor is willing to throw anyone he wants to in jail."

Yes! Jean thought. Finally, someone else was starting to see through Magnus's "upstanding leader" charade. Part of her wanted to go straight to that group and tell them they were right.

But as long as Magnus had Micah in his clutches, she couldn't risk openly rousing more opposition. What she really needed was Dr. Fields's antidote. She needed to wake the adults before Micah's trial—before Magnus could rig the jury and set Micah adrift on an ice floe.

Her brother's life depended on her getting that formula. And her last chance to get it was sitting at a table in the corner with a stuffed narwhal.

Leaning on her crutch, Jean shuffled in that direction. "Hi," she said, pulling out the chair opposite Cora. "Can I sit here?"

Cora sniffed. "I'd rather you not. That's Spike's chair."

Jean glanced down. The stuffed narwhal was perched on the seat.

"Oh—sorry, Spike!" she said. "I'll stand." If groveling to Cora's toy was the only way to get information about—and hopefully from—Micah, she would do it.

Jean heard a soft *baaah!* as Katrin and Rambo approached. "Hey, is he okay?" Katrin asked.

"Yes, he's very comfortable," Cora replied, and Jean breathed a sigh of relief. "Though the table's squashing his horn a little."

Now Jean had to struggle to maintain her self-control. "Not *Spike,*" she said through gritted teeth. "Micah. My *brother.* Is he okay?"

"Oh!" Cora cried. "Yes. Micah is in good spirits. Though he didn't like Spike's suggestion that we ask for a please bargain."

"A what?"

"A please bargain. It's where you say, 'Please, Mr. Judge, I didn't do the really bad crime. But I did do the smaller crime, so can't you just punish me for that?' "

Katrin raised an eyebrow. "You mean a *plea* bargain?" When they had TV reception in the summer, Katrin and her mom watched a lot of *COI: Clues on Ice,* a courtroom show set in the capital.

"That's what I said: a please bargain!" Cora shuffled her papers importantly. "But he won't do it. Mama always complains that her clients make things difficult for themselves. Now Spike and I know what she means."

Jean might have laughed—if her brother's survival wasn't at stake. "So if he won't do the . . . bargain," she said, "what's your strategy?"

"Witnesses," Cora said. "And testimonies, and objections and sustaineds. No overruleds. Getting overruled is bad, right, Spike?"

The narwhal did not respond.

What little faith Jean might have had in Cora's lawyering ability was fading fast. "Okay," she said, "those are good words, but—"

"Thank you!" Cora interrupted. "Mama says using big words is half of lawyering."

"And what's the other half?" Katrin asked.

"Hmm . . . I don't know! I'll have to ask her when she wakes up."

This was Micah's counsel for the trial.

"Look, Cora . . . ," Jean said, lowering her voice. "Did Micah . . . give you any kind of message? For me? Like, maybe . . ." She wanted to say "a formula," but stopped herself. Spies might be listening, and she didn't know that Cora could be trusted, either.

"Nope," Cora said. "And even if he did, I'm not supposed to carry notes between you. Sorry."

It sounded like Micah didn't quite trust Cora, either. That was probably wise of him, but still . . . they were so close to ending the hibernation! If only Cora *could* carry notes between them. If only . . .

The solution came to her. "Hey, thanks! I need to get back to work in the kitchen."

"Yes," Cora said, "and Spike and I need to start drafting our arguments. I'm doing the opening, and he'll do the closing."

Katrin looked appalled. With any luck, though, those arguments would never need to happen. Jean leaned on her crutch and began to move away.

"What's going on?" Katrin whispered, catching up with her.

"No time—I'll tell you later!"

Jean went through the pantry, gathering rice noodles and peanuts as fast as she could with her free hand. She dumped the ingredients on the counter and looked for goose meat, scallions, and bean sprouts in the refrigerator.

By the time she made it back to the counter, her knee was starting to throb again. She ignored it. Magnus had said that they could bring Micah food. The dish she would cook for him needed to tell him that she was sorry and she loved him and she would make things right. But it also, quite literally, needed to ask:

What's the secret formula?

The pad thai Isara had cooked the other day had featured long noodles in a thin but sticky sauce. She could use those noodles to spell out her question, and Micah could use them to send her an answer!

Jean set a large pot of water to boil, then pulled out a cleaver and began to hack the meat into stir-fry-ready slices.

Isara appeared beside her at the counter. She waited to

be yelled at for touching his pots, but he simply pulled another knife out of the block and chopped scallions. Jean nodded gratefully, then put Isara's huge wok on a burner and splashed oil into it.

They cooked, and she whispered her plan to him. When the food was ready, he brought out a beautiful black porcelain plate with a matching domed lid for the food.

"This way, you'll have an excuse to wait at the station for his reply—because you need to get our dish back."

It was a great idea. Jean took the plate and carefully spelled out her question in saucy noodles. She then scattered the meat, vegetables, and peanuts over them, covering her words just enough that, she hoped, no one would catch on even if a guard peeked at the food before it got to Micah.

A few minutes later, Axel helped Jean into the snowplow. She had to bring Micah the dish herself. Even if he couldn't see her, maybe, somehow, he would sense that she was in the building with him.

The police station was empty except for Bartleby, who was tipping back precariously in the deputy's chair.

"We could take him," Axel whispered. "Two against one."

Jean shook her head slightly. Police backup was always nearby.

Bartleby sat up as they approached his desk. "The prisoner isn't allowed any visitors!"

"We're just here to deliver food," Axel said.

Jean's heart squeezed as she held up the black platter.

"What is it?" Bartleby leaned forward.

"Pad thai," she said, "and it's getting cold. Magnus promised that my brother would be treated well here—he should be able to eat his meals while they're still hot."

Bartleby lifted the plate out of Jean's hands, and a thrill ran through her. The plan was working!

Except that he just stood there. "And what about us police?" He glanced back at the half-eaten cheese-and-jam sandwich on his desk. "You promised to bring me fried bananas."

Jean gaped at him. "That was before your sister *kneecapped* me, and before you *arrested my brother*!"

He shrugged. "If I can't have bananas, I guess I'll have to help myself to some of this." And he yanked the cover off the platter, dug in with the enclosed fork, and brought a huge bite of pad thai to his mouth.

The squeezing in Jean's chest grew tighter with each bite Bartleby took. Finally, he replaced the dome on the dish and picked it up.

"You two stay right there, or the rest of this might end up on the floor." And he disappeared through the heavy back door.

The message was ruined. Jean dug her fists into her pockets, willing herself not to cry.

"Now what?" Axel asked.

She sank onto one of the hard-backed chairs by the station's door. "I guess . . . we wait for the plate and try again tomorrow."

But tomorrow was Friday—one day before Micah's trial and the election. Even if they got the formula from him tomorrow, that wouldn't leave much time to make a plan and wake the sleepers.

Jean thought over their situation. Magnus had switched the livers to cause the great hibernation. And he was taking advantage of all their parents being asleep to manipulate the kids into voting for the thistleberry plant.

But *why*? Sure, the Kings' money was tied up in the plant, but Jean didn't believe that money alone was enough to make Magnus break so many rules. He *loved* rules. Maybe this was about pleasing his father; if Magnus could pass the bill that his father couldn't, he would be a hero to his family.

Jean hated to admit it, but she understood that. When she'd taken her secret trip to Bigsby, she'd wanted to help people, but she'd also wanted the glory of waking the sleepers. A medal being hung around her neck. And, most importantly, her parents standing there, pride filling their hearts just like it had when Micah played Captain Polonius on Founders' Day.

Maybe, underneath it all, she and Magnus were after the same thing.

But that didn't make what he had done right. And there was only one way out of this mess: Get the antidote formula and wake the adults *before* the trial and election. The thistleberry plant plan would be voted down—and a real judge would dismiss the case against Micah.

The heavy door swung open and Bartleby emerged, plate in hand. "Your brother sure is a slow eater. I've never seen anyone who likes to play with his food so much."

At least jail hadn't broken Micah's spirit. At home, Mom

was always telling him to stop making structures out of his vegetables and just eat them.

Jean took the dish back from Bartleby and peeked under the dome. Micah hadn't quite eaten everything. A shape caught her eye: a shriveled noodle stuck to the plate in a figure eight. And the noodle to its left made a straight number 1.

Cracking the dome open wider, Jean stared in. There, above the numbers, were noodles shaped like letters, and to the right of the figure eight was a slash of bean sprout and two bits of peanut that looked like a percentage sign.

Jean's heart soared, but before Bartleby could catch on, she slammed the dome back down over the plate.

Enough of her question must have gotten through. Micah had sent her Dr. Fields's antidote formula, spelled out in his leftovers.

CHAPTER 24

Back at the restaurant, Jean and Axel whispered the good news to Katrin and Isara. Later, when they met at the salon, she yanked the dome off the plate. “Do I have the smartest brother in the world, or what?”

Everyone crowded around. “Clever,” Katrin said. “Micah’s lucky that Bartleby was too thick to catch on.”

Jean snorted. “He was probably too busy digesting stolen food.”

"Speaking of food," Isara said. "I brought more snacks."

Once everyone had helped themselves to vegetable skewers and thick, peanutty satay sauce, it was time to get down to business.

"Okay, so the 'Fat, 18%' part is pretty clear," Katrin said. "And, Jean, based on what he told you before he got arrested, it should be a solution, right?"

Jean nodded.

"That means something that contains eighteen percent fat," Katrin said. "And in his noodle-message he told us how much to give people—one fluid ounce of solution per forty pounds of body weight."

"So what are we waiting for?" Axel asked. "Let's start waking people!"

But Jean held up a hand. "Wait. What should we make the solution out of? And how are we supposed to give it to the sleepers?"

Axel groaned. "I thought we were close."

"We are!" Jean said. "We'll just have to experiment."

"Experiment?" Isara asked. "On the sleepers?"

Katrin shook her head. "The sleepers are under twenty-four-hour guard now by Magnus's goons. Remember?"

"Also, a human subject is supposed to give consent before you can experiment on them," Jean said. "Dr. Fields is always strict about that."

"Yeah, well, I think we could break that rule today," Axel grumbled. "It's kind of an emergency."

"Better," Jean said, "would be for one of *us* to volunteer

to be a test subject." She'd been pondering this ever since she'd seen Micah's message. "I think it should be me."

Katrin's shadowed eyes popped open. "You? Jean, what are you talking about?"

Jean took a deep breath. "We need to figure this out," she said. "Fast. If we can put me into hibernation and then test the cure out on me, we'll know if it's worked! Plus, I'm of age, so I'm old enough to eat the liver—really eat it this time—if I want to."

She reached into her backpack and pulled out an almost-empty plastic bag. "I asked Katrin to take this out of the freezer as soon as she got home from dinner," she told everyone. "It's almost defrosted, and there's one portion left." She unzipped the bag and gently shook its contents onto one of the plates Isara had set out for snacks. It jiggled and glistened under the bright overhead lights of the salon.

"Jean, this is nuts!" Katrin blurted. "If I'd known that *this* was your idea, I would never have defrosted that liver bite. I've lost my mom to this hibernation, and we've lost Micah to jail. I can't risk losing my best friend, too!"

Rambo tucked his head under Katrin's hand; she stroked his wool, but kept her gaze on Jean. "Don't do this. Please."

"I agree," Isara said. "There has to be another way."

"Yeah," Axel said. "You're too important to this operation. If you need a test subject, it can be me."

"You're too young," Jean said.

"Then I'll be the subject," Isara said.

"But you haven't eaten meat in years," Axel protested. "And who'll cook for us if you don't wake up?"

"Let me do it," Katrin said. "My job's not essential."

Jean shook her head. "You're not old enough to consent, either."

"Well, *someone* has to eat it," Axel said. "Can we draw straws?"

"That's fair," Isara said.

Jean knew she was outnumbered. Katrin rummaged around in a drawer and returned with four hair curlers: three pink and one green, all the same shape and size. "Whoever draws the green curler will eat the liver," she said. "But not until we've weighed you and mixed up an antidote, of course. Safety first, agreed?"

"Agreed," said Isara.

"Agreed," said Axel.

"Agreed," sighed Jean.

Katrin threw the curlers into Jean's empty backpack, and they all plunged their hands in. But as Jean's fingers brushed a curler, Katrin screamed.

"Rambo! NO!"

Jean spun around to see the very last bite of high-altitude bear liver disappear into Rambo's mouth.

She dove for the plate, but it was too late. Every last trace of liver had been licked up.

"What in the name of St. Polonius?" Axel yelped. "I thought sheep were vegetarians!"

"Nonononononono." Jean buried her head in her hands. Why hadn't she watched Rambo? She knew he liked to go after the human snacks. She *knew*! Their experiment was ruined . . . and what would happen to the sheep? She thought of her silent promise to Micah to take care of Rambo.

She took a deep breath and peeked out from behind her hands. Rambo was still clip-clopping around the room as if nothing had happened. Katrin was even grinning.

"This is perfect!" Katrin said. "I mean, I'm generally against animal testing, but in this case, a subject has pretty much fallen into our laps!"

Jean blinked. "You think this is a *good* thing?"

"At least we all get to stay awake," Axel said.

Isara glanced over at Rambo, now chewing on a wicker wastebasket. "*He* seems to be wide awake, too."

"Well, think back to Founders' Day," Katrin said. "It was almost an hour before most people started to pass out, remember?"

Jean felt like hot lava was rising in her chest. "So we're just supposed to sit around here and wait for Micah's favorite sheep to collapse? What if thistleberry toxins work differently in sheep than in humans? What if we can't test the antidote on him? And . . ." Jean couldn't even bring herself to say the next part out loud: *What if the poison kills him?*

Her knee spasmed as she scrambled to her feet. Katrin rushed over to help her. "Oh, Jean—we're not going to let anything bad happen to Rambo. We'll all stay and watch him, and the moment he goes into hibernation, we'll be ready with the treatment. Come on—we'll start mixing up a solution right now."

Axel and Isara nodded their agreement, but Jean wasn't

ready to be calmed. "What solution?" she snapped, stepping back. "I was going to wait to eat the liver until we had a treatment ready! But we don't even know what it should be made of—and it's not like we can just mix oil and water together. How will we keep the fat from separating out?"

"Fair question," Katrin said.

"Wait!" Isara's black eyes were suddenly bright. "I think— There's something— The restaurant— Hang on!" He snatched his coat and dashed out of the shop.

A couple of minutes later, he was back. "I was right!" he panted, icy chunks sliding off his coat. "Look: eighteen percent fat!"

He was holding out a can. Jean brushed the snow off the label.

Top-grade, extra-thick, preservative-free coconut milk. Imported from Thailand.

"Look at the nutrition facts!" Isara said. "A serving is one hundred grams, and there are eighteen grams of fat per serving. That's eighteen percent!"

"And it's emulsified," Jean said. "That means the fat is suspended evenly throughout the liquid."

"Oh, bravo, Isara!" Katrin cried. "This is exactly what we need!"

Isara beamed. "I have a shelf loaded with these at the restaurant. My parents had them shipped from Thailand and trucked in from the capital before the pass closed."

"You're sure we can use up your stock?" Jean asked him. "This milk is special to your family."

"Of course I'm sure," Isara said. "My parents will be happy to take curries off the menu this winter if it means we can all be awake and together again."

"Okay." Jean clapped her hands. "Then we've got some coconut milk to measure out."

CHAPTER 25

It took only forty-five minutes for Rambo to show signs of poisoning. One moment he was trotting around; the next, he had slumped onto the floor in a wooly heap, his thick-lashed eyes drooping shut.

"Ohhhh-kay!" Axel cried. "It's showtime!"

The first thing they had to do was weigh Rambo so they could calculate how much coconut milk to use as an antidote. Katrin set her bathroom scale up next to the sheep, and the four of them heaved him onto it.

When the number popped up on the scale, Isara gasped. "One hundred three pounds? I didn't know sheep got so big!"

"He's our prize ram." Jean stroked Rambo's wool.

"It's good that he weighs so much," Katrin said. "Closer to the weight of an adult human. He'll be a good test case."

"So how're we gonna get the coconut milk into him?" Axel asked.

"I know!" Katrin darted into the salon's back room and returned with a clear plastic squirt bottle. "A hair dye bottle," she said. "Meant for coloring, but this one's never been used. And see, it even has measurement markings on it, in fluid ounces."

Axel frowned. "So you're gonna squirt the milk into Rambo's fleece?"

Katrin gave him a withering look. "No, squid-brain. We'll get him to *drink* out of the bottle."

Could sheep drink in their sleep? Could people? Jean had seen half-asleep baby lambs nurse, so maybe this could work.

Katrin stood at the hair-washing sink, carefully tipping the contents of a can of coconut milk into the open hair dye bottle. "Jean, help me with the math. One hundred three pounds, and one ounce per forty pounds, is . . ."

"A drop over two and a half ounces," Jean said.

"Great. Aaand, there!" Katrin screwed the squirty top back onto the bottle. The thick liquid sloshed gently as she carried it to Jean. "It's your family's sheep," she said. "Would you like to do the honors?"

"Uh, sure." Jean took the bottle as the others slid Rambo off the scale and onto a waiting towel, laying him on his side.

"Rambo . . . ," she coaxed. "I've got something here that'll make you feel better." She slipped the bottle's nozzle between his lips, then waited. He was still breathing through his nose—that was good. Jean gave the bottle a squeeze.

Would he just drool it back out? Or worse, choke on it? She leaned in so close that Rambo could have kissed her forehead. What was going on in there?

Then she saw a movement in his throat, accompanied by the faintest *"Glug."* She pulled the bottle out and checked it—just under two ounces remained. She pried the sheep's teeth carefully apart and looked deep into his mouth.

"He drank it!"

Axel and Isara whooped, and Katrin squeezed Jean's shoulder. Jean reinserted the nozzle into Rambo's mouth and squeezed the bottle again. Again, he swallowed. Slowly and carefully, she fed him the rest.

"How long," Isara asked, "do we think it'll take to work?"

"Hard to know," Jean said. "But maybe the same amount of time it took the poison to work?"

At first, everyone sat in a circle around Rambo, until Katrin insisted that staring at him wasn't doing anyone any good. She made them move to the other side of the room, where they reheated Isara's snacks under one of the hair dryers and picked at them. Nobody was hungry.

At forty-two minutes, Rambo was still a wooly, unconscious lump on the floor.

"What will we do if this doesn't work?" Jean burst out.

"It *will* work," Katrin said. "We did the calculations correctly."

"Yeah, but . . . what if Dr. Fields's formula was off? She was still testing it. Or what if Micah misremembered it? Or what if one of his noodles shifted, and we read the percentages wrong??" Jean felt the panic rising in her voice, but she couldn't help it. "There are *so* many ways that we could have messed it up." She glanced at the clock—forty-four minutes gone by. "We should start working on a backup plan."

Axel had wandered over to Katrin's mom's haircutting station and picked up a cordless razor from her table. "Cool," he said, holding it up. "I bet this could do some damage."

"Put that back!" Katrin called over her shoulder.

But Axel continued to twirl it between his hands. "Jean's right," he said. "What if this whole antidote thing doesn't work out? The trial could get ugly. It's probably best to arm ourselves. Too bad no one grabbed that doctor-girl's scalpel." He looked up at Katrin. "How many more of these power switchblades have you got?"

"That's not a switchblade, chum lump!" Katrin advanced on him. "And no one's 'arming' anyone! If you show up at Micah's trial with a weapon, Magnus'll maroon you so fast—"

"As *if*—"

As their arguing grew louder, Isara grabbed Jean's sleeve. "Did you hear that? Quiet, you two! The sheep made a noise!"

Jean dashed across the floor and skidded to kneel by Rambo's side, the throbbing in her knee forgotten as she threw her arms around him. The sheep opened his eyes, let out a soft *baaah,* and threw up right in Jean's lap.

Jean sobbed and hugged Rambo tighter. She had never been so happy to be near a sheep—to smell its foul breath in her face, to be covered in its puke. Rambo was awake! They might have a shot at waking the other sleepers. The election was not lost; Micah was not doomed.

Rambo gave her a gentle nip on the shoulder, and she finally released him. He clambered to his feet and made a beeline for the warmed-up snacks.

Everyone cheered. Axel and Katrin even hugged. Jean grabbed a hair towel and wiped off her pants before pushing herself to her feet.

"On to phase two," she announced, "wake up the humans!"

"To town hall!" Isara cried.

"But Magnus has armed guards watching the sleepers," Katrin reminded them.

"So what?" Axel asked. "Once we tell them we've found a cure, I'm sure they'll want us to come in."

But Jean wasn't. "I don't know," she said. "Remember, Magnus wants our parents to stay asleep. He wants *kids* to vote in the election on Saturday, not adults. I'm sure he told the guards that their duty was to stop anyone from 'messing' with the sleepers. But the truth is that the kids are guarding everyone against getting a cure, too, even if they don't know it."

Axel's face fell; so did Isara's. "So you think the guards won't let us in to wake up our parents?" Isara asked.

"What I'm saying," Jean said, "is that we have to be strategic. If we can come up with a way to distract the guards—to get them away from their posts—we'll have a better shot."

"The trial!" Katrin said. "We can do it during the trial!"

Everyone leaned in to listen to her.

"Magnus said Micah's trial would be open to the public, right? He said a jury would be selected from Micah's peers. That means everyone will have to show up in the courtroom at the same time to be considered. Even the guards—even B&B."

"Even *us,*" Jean pointed out. "And anyway, waiting until Micah's trial to start waking the sleepers up is cutting things awfully close, isn't it?" She'd been counting on adults to stop the trial from happening.

"Trials take hours, Jean, or days," Katrin said. "And the courtroom is just a floor above the sleepers' room. It's the only way for us to get in there without raising suspicion." Katrin grinned. "A surprise attack—Magnus'll never see it coming! Imagine his face when a couple hundred adults and teenagers storm into his courtroom to put a stop to things."

Katrin continued, elaborating on how they might sneak down and wake the sleepers during the trial. But as she talked, an alternative plan was taking shape in Jean's head—a plan she was shocked she hadn't thought of sooner. "Wait!" she cried. "What about *my* parents? They're the only adults not under guard—they're out at the farmhouse. Axel, you could drive us all there right now to wake them up!"

Heat was rising in her chest. She didn't need to wake the whole town to give Magnus the shock of his life; her furious mother, barging into the mayor-boy's office, would do quite well enough.

But Axel shook his head. "Jean, I tried to go out there yesterday morning," he said. "I thought you and Micah would want me to check up on your folks. But the snow has piled up like *crazy*. I'm sure my dad could maneuver through it, but I'm not that good yet. I pushed as far as I could, but I didn't even make it a mile up the road. I'm sorry."

Jean tried not to let her disappointment show. "It's not your fault, Axel. You weren't ready for your job—like all of us. That's why we *have* to wake our parents. But thanks for trying."

Axel tipped an imaginary cap at her just as Katrin whirled to face the window. "What was that? I heard something."

Isara rushed over and peered into the darkness. "I can't see."

"Hang on." Katrin turned on the salon's outside light. No one was there. But then Axel gasped and darted outside to scoop something shiny out of the snow.

He ran back in. "Look!" He held out a temporary police badge.

"And there are footprints," Isara said. Sure enough, fresh prints dotted the snow, running from the salon in the direction of town hall.

"Bloody whale blubber," Katrin cursed. "A spy! How long do you think they were out there? What did they *hear*?"

Jean wasn't willing to wait for half of Magnus's police force to show up to find out. "Go home!" she said. "Everyone, go home, and if anyone asks, you were there all night. This meeting never happened."

Isara and Axel grabbed their coats and fled; Katrin wrangled Rambo, shut off all the lights, and helped Jean up the stairs to her apartment.

Jean hardly slept, half expecting fists to pound on Katrin's door. But nobody came. Was it possible that the spy hadn't seen much? In this weather, it was too cold to stand outside for very long. Maybe he or she had only been there for a couple of minutes, and missed Rambo's miraculous resurrection. Maybe Magnus would stay in the dark about their plan.

Jean had to hope so. It was Friday morning now. Who knew what could happen in twenty-four hours?

YOU ARE INVITED TO A TRIAL . . .
AND AN ELECTION

Come do your civic duty for the town of St. Polonius-on-the-Fjord!*

SATURDAY, OCTOBER 21

Jury selection for the trial of Micah Huddy (on counts of espionage, high treason, and breaking and entering) will start at precisely 9 a.m. All citizens of St. Polonius are excused from work and day care and asked** instead to appear at town hall, courtroom 1, to participate and bear witness. Box lunches will be provided by Tasty Thai Hut. Election to commence immediately after lunch.

BE READY TO VOTE!***

* Attendance is mandatory.
** Actually, required.
*** If you are still not sure how to vote on the thistleberry plant, please see Mayor Magnus King or one of his associates for free guidance!

CHAPTER 26

"Have you seen this?" Isara waved a freshly printed flyer in Jean's face.

Mostly, Jean was relieved to see *him* in the kitchen, as well as Axel in the dining room. Magnus hadn't sent his goons out last night for anyone. But as Jean took the paper from Isara, her good mood darkened.

"Magnus printed up invitations to Micah's trial? Like it's some sort of public festival?"

"Yes," Isara said, "and look at this!" He pointed to a line near the bottom. "*Box lunches will be provided by Tasty Thai Hut.* Magnus didn't even ask me—he just assumed. As if I don't already have enough work to do!"

Jean raised her eyebrows. She was much more concerned about Micah than extra cooking. In fact—

"Isara, maybe the box lunches are a good thing."

He snorted. "How?"

The night before, at the salon, they hadn't had time to figure out how they would smuggle all the coconut milk they needed into town hall on Saturday. If the average sleeper weighed one hundred fifty pounds, they would need 3.75 ounces of coconut milk, meaning that one can only held enough to wake about four people. And since there were two hundred and fifty sleepers in that room, they would need to bring sixty-three cans—way more than four kids could sneak in under their coats.

"Tomorrow," she said, "you can show up early with a bunch of boxes, claiming they're full of lunch. But if they're filled with coconut milk, we can sneak the cure in right under everybody's noses!"

Isara smiled. "That *is* a good idea."

The morning passed more quickly than Jean had expected. Her knee was still sore, so Katrin and Axel took turns helping her bring meals to the police station for Micah. Again, none of them was allowed to see him. But no more messages made of leftover food came back, so at least Jean was able to assume that Micah was eating enough.

As she moved around the dining room at lunchtime,

helping serve Isara's khao pad fried rice, she kept her ears open for any more anti-Magnus rumblings. But no one was complaining openly. The only talk she heard was about the big vote. Some of the younger kids seemed to be under the impression that their TV and Internet service would magically return the moment the thistleberry bill passed.

"These kids are in for a rude awakening," Katrin muttered as Jean arrived at her table. Micah's spot was conspicuously empty, his chair stolen by a former floor-sitter. Rambo baaed from below the table, nipping at people's legs and generally exhibiting no lasting effects from his adventures in hibernation the night before.

"Well, their parents are definitely in for an awakening," Jean whispered back, "though it could be rude for *us* if they all throw up like Rambo did." Thankfully, Katrin had lent Jean clean cargo pants to wear today.

"Ugh," Katrin said. "Maybe we should bring barf buckets."

"No room," Jean said. "But please bring all the hair dye bottles you can find!"

Katrin smuggled the bottles over after lunch, taking care to avoid the half-hourly patrol of Skiff Alley by one of Magnus's new guards. Jean and Isara filled them with coconut milk and packed them into boxes labeled "trial lunches." Jean had another good idea: making sandwiches to scatter on top of the bottles, in case a guard decided to check inside. "And besides," she added, "the sleepers'll probably be hungry when they wake up. Rambo sure was."

"That animal is always hungry," Isara said.

• • •

After dinner that night, Jean and Isara locked their boxes in the restaurant's pantry; then Jean went to the salon alone. It was too dangerous for the group to meet again, but Jean had let Axel know where to pick them up the next day with his truck.

She found Katrin in the middle of the salon floor, circling Rambo with a hair dryer and fluffing up his newly trimmed wool.

"Jean!" Katrin switched the dryer off. "I hope you don't mind. I was feeling a little nervous, and styling calms me down."

Jean smiled. "No problem—Rambo was getting tangly. He looks great now! Clean and . . . symmetrical."

"Not totally symmetrical," Katrin said. "Come see." Jean approached, and saw that one side of Rambo indeed did not match the other. Two words had been shaved into his right flank: *ST. RAMBO*. And two different ones were shaved into his left: *SOME SHEEP*.

"Because he is," Katrin said, low. "If he hadn't eaten the liver last night, we wouldn't be ready to wake all the sleepers up tomorrow. He's a true hero of this town!"

"St. Rambo," Jean said with a smile. "Micah'll like that."

Katrin yanked the hair dryer cord from its outlet and started to wind it up. "Isn't it strange," she said, "to think that after tomorrow, everything will be back to normal? School will reopen, and my mom will go back to doing everyone's hair." She sounded a bit wistful.

"Hey," Jean said softly. "You're gonna make a terrific hair artist when you're older—the best in the North Country. People will come from Bigsby—no, all the way from the capital!—just to get an appointment with you."

Katrin grinned. "You think? Of course I won't take any Bigsbyans—not after the way they treated you and Isara when you tried to sail over for help."

But Jean shrugged. "We probably shouldn't judge everyone in Bigsby based on one stupid boat captain's actions," she said. "Imagine if Magnus was the only St. Polonian someone had ever met. What kind of impression would they have of us?"

"Ugh," Katrin said. "Good point."

"And if the weather hadn't stopped us from sailing again," Jean continued, "maybe I would have found someone in Bigsby to help."

"Yeah, but you didn't need to," Katrin said. "You figured it all out by yourself in the end." She grabbed a broom to sweep up the fluffy tufts of Rambo-wool that were floating around the room. "It's kind of funny when you think about it—out of all of us, you're the one who's worked the hardest to wake the grown-ups, when you're probably the one person who was best equipped to take charge of things without them."

"What?" Katrin had it all wrong. "You and Axel and Isara, you've been running entire businesses. I've barely learned how to brew a pitcher of tea!"

Katrin paused mid-sweep. "Jean. You saved us. You saved this *town*. Or you will have, anyway, after tomorrow." She resumed her sweeping with more force. "Forget St. Rambo and St. Polonius—soon everyone's gonna be talking about St. Jean."

Jean had to laugh. She hadn't accomplished anything, except getting Micah thrown in jail. "There's a lot left to do."

Now Katrin laughed nervously. "I know." Last night, up in the apartment, they'd agreed that while Jean was keeping an eye on Micah's trial the next day, Katrin would slip out of the courtroom with Isara and Axel and lead the troops through the secret rescue effort downstairs. It was a lot of responsibility . . . and Jean could tell that Katrin wasn't one hundred percent confident she could do it.

Katrin emptied her dustpan and reached to flick off the salon's light.

But before the bulbs winked out, Jean caught sight of Katrin's mom's workstation. The cordless razor—the one Axel had been playing with the night before—was gone.

"Hey," Jean said, "where's that razor that was here yesterday? Did you use it on Rambo?"

"What? No, I used the plug-in kind on him—more power. But the other one must be around somewhere."

Katrin didn't sound worried, but a shiver of dread passed through Jean. Had Axel pocketed the razor when no one was looking? Was he planning to go all Captain Polonius on Magnus's liver with it tomorrow if their plan didn't work out?

Don't be paranoid! she told herself. Their plan *would* work, and there would be no reason for Axel to get violent.

"You coming up?" Katrin asked.

"Yeah." Jean reached for Katrin's hand and gave it a

squeeze. "We're all going to do a great job tomorrow," she said, trying to sound strong.

They had to.

Isara tried to get Jean to eat a bowl of rice porridge the next morning, but she couldn't get a bite down. "Sorry," she told him. "I'm sure it's very good."

"At least drink this, then," he said. "I made one for each of us—full strength this time, extra energy guaranteed."

He passed Jean a mug filled with reddish-brown liquid, and she took it with both hands; her knee was better today, so she didn't need her crutch. She sipped; the tea was more bitter *and* more sweet than usual. She sucked it down in long gulps.

Twenty minutes later, as she watched her friends heave heavy boxes of coconut milk and sandwiches into Axel's truck, Jean felt like her heart might pound right out of her chest. Maybe a mega-dose of caffeine and sugar hadn't been such a good breakfast choice.

Once the truck was loaded, Axel drove them to town hall. Just for today, Rambo was closed up in Katrin's sheep-proofed apartment.

The side entrance to town hall was guarded by two of Magnus's police recruits. One was Ben Hansen, his spiky new haircut now matched by the spiky ball on a chain—a flail—that he held in his gloved hand. And the other was Alaria Daly, who had nearly run Jean over on her skateboard that first day at the Tasty Thai Hut. But today, instead of fairy wings, a loaded crossbow was strapped to her back.

"See," Axel muttered. "I told you we should have armed ourselves."

Does that mean he didn't *take the razor?* Jean wondered.

Katrin jumped in. "There isn't going to be *any* conflict. And Isara does the talking, like we agreed."

They approached the guards. "You can't come in here," Alaria said. "Everyone has to enter through the main doors at eight forty-five."

Isara plastered on a wide smile. "But we're catering," he said, holding out a copy of Magnus's "invitation." "I'm the interim owner and head chef of the Tasty Thai Hut, and these are my assistants. We need to bring the lunches into the building."

Ben took the flier from Isara, then glanced down at the labeled boxes that they were carrying. He looked over at Alaria, who shrugged. "I guess that's okay." He took a key off his belt loop to open the door. "What are we having for lunch, anyway?"

"None of your business," Axel snapped, Katrin's elbow to his side coming too late to shut him up.

"What he means," Katrin said quickly, "is that it's a surprise."

"Ooh," Alaria said, "is it those tasty noodles again? The ones with the peanuts?"

"You'll see," Isara said, and they heaved their boxes through the doorway.

Jean spotted a bathroom sign. "The sleepers are in the

room across from the bathrooms!" she whispered. Amazingly, no one was guarding that door—but if the building was locked, she supposed there was no need. She led the way, and soon their boxes were piled up right outside the sleeping-room door. She tested the knob. *Whew*—unlocked. Snores rose from inside.

We could go in right now, Jean thought. *Go in and start waking everyone up.*

"Hey, what's taking so long?" Alaria called. "We didn't say you could stay!"

"Come on," Katrin muttered. "They'll be in the courtroom soon enough, and our path will be clear."

Back outside, a crowd was gathering on the town hall steps as thick flakes tumbled from the slate-gray sky. On the square in front of the building, Founders' Day tents (which normally would have been packed away by now) sagged under the weight of the snow that had been falling all week.

"Make way!" a booming voice shouted. "Prisoner coming through!"

The crowd on the steps parted for Magnus, who strolled up at a measured pace. Behind him came Bertha and Bartleby, elbows firmly crooked around Micah's. He was still in the clothes and boots he'd been wearing at his arrest on Thursday, and his hands were again tied behind his back. He looked pale and haggard, but at least he was walking on his own, and Jean didn't spot any bruises.

Micah's eyes scanned the crowd and finally he spotted her. "Jeannie!"

She took a step toward him, but Bertha raised her night-stick. "No one communicates with the prisoner!"

Jean's knee wobbled at the sight of the weapon, though she wasn't afraid of being beaten anymore. What she *did* fear was getting herself locked up somewhere during the trial. She needed to be in that courtroom, to make sure that Micah was okay and that the others had enough time in the sleepers' room below. She couldn't get in trouble.

She took a step back, and while it pierced her heart, she shifted her gaze away from Micah. It was the only way she could keep from running to him.

JURY SLIP

Please fill out in full.

First name: ______________________

Last name: ______________________

Do you solemnly swear to uphold the law as set forth in our nation's constitution & the St. Polonius-on-the-Fjord town charter? (circle one)

yes no

Signature:

____

CHAPTER 27

The town hall's front doors opened, and everyone streamed in.

"You all need to register!" a door guard shouted. "We need to check that everyone is here, and make a record of which adult you'll be replacing as a voter or juror! Please fill out a slip to put yourself into the jury pool!"

"What a joke," Katrin said into Jean's ear. "As if Magnus would let the jury members be selected randomly! Not one friend of Micah's will end up on that jury."

Finally, they moved in out of the cold. Long tables lined both sides of the lobby.

Jean and her friends headed to the nearest table, where Liddy Dowell presided. "Last name?" she asked Isara.

"Ratana," he said, and she made a tick on her clipboard.

"What adult are you here to represent?" she asked.

"I suppose my father, Adipat Ratana."

"You're the oldest male child in your family?"

Isara nodded. "The only child."

Another check. "Okay. Write your name on this slip of paper for the jury pool, then go to the courtroom on the second floor."

Isara handed in his slip, and Liddy dropped it into one of the same silver bowls that had held liver on Founders' Day. Katrin and Axel followed, and then it was Jean's turn. "I'm here to represent Ingrid Huddy," she told Liddy as she filled out her slip. "And when the time comes to vote, Micah will represent our father, Brian Huddy."

Liddy gave her a cool stare. "I'm sorry," she said, "but convicted felons lose their right to participate in elections."

"He's not convicted!" Jean snapped.

"Yet."

Katrin grabbed Jean's hand. "Come on—let's get good seats."

Liddy stared after them as Jean let Katrin pull her away. "It won't matter," Katrin whispered as they mounted the stairs. "The adults will be awake before the trial's half over. None of us are going to vote!"

In the courtroom, the rows of seats up close to the judge's

podium were already full. Jean and the crew planned to sit near the room's exit so Axel, Isara, and Katrin could slip out once the trial got underway. If everyone in town was required to attend the trial, then there shouldn't be any guards in the halls—but if there were, Isara would say that he needed Katrin and Axel's help setting up lunch.

At the front of the room, Micah sat behind a table with one hand tied to his chair and his half-lawyer next to him. Cora was swimming in one of her mother's suit jackets, and on the table next to her, Spike wore a pair of black-rimmed eyeglasses. Behind the table next to them sat Francis Bosco, the eleven-year-old son of the town prosecutor. And

climbing into the judge's chair in Judge Barrett's billowing black robes was Magnus.

Jean watched as Magnus reached into his robes and pulled out a walkie-talkie. He said something into it, then held it up to his ear. As he listened, his eyes grazed the crowd until they landed on Jean's row.

He continued to stare, his mouth curling into a smile. Then he spoke into the walkie-talkie again, never letting his gaze waver.

The air in the courtroom suddenly felt hot and thick. Who was Magnus talking to? "Guys," Jean whispered as loudly as she dared, "something's going on. Maybe Magnus does know more about our plans than we—"

But the rest of her sentence was buried under a series of thumps that echoed throughout the courtroom. Magnus was rapping the podium with a judge's gavel.

"Hear ye, hear ye! All rise! This court is in session!"

One hundred kids shuffled to their feet, and the courtroom door slammed shut. The trial was starting.

Magnus drew himself up to his full height. "According to the laws of this country—and, of course, the town charter of St. Polonius-on-the-Fjord—all accused criminals have the right to be tried by a jury of their peers. Therefore, we will begin today by selecting, at random, seven citizens to sit in judgment of the accused. Ms. Dowell, will you bring forth the names?"

Liddy scurried forward with the silver bowl full of slips.

"If your name is called," Magnus announced, "and

neither attorney objects to your serving as a juror, then you must come forward immediately and take a seat on the jury bench."

He plunged a hand into the bowl and drew out the first name.

"Axel Gorson!"

"Huh?" Axel blurted. The crowd laughed, and Katrin cursed under her breath. Jean stared up at Magnus.

"Defender Buggins," Magnus said, turning to Micah's lawyer. "Do you have any objection to this young man serving on the jury?"

Cora bent down briefly to confer with Spike, then straightened. "Nope!"

"That should be 'Nope, Your Honor,'" Magnus reminded her.

"Oh, sorry. Nope, Your Honor!"

Magnus turned toward Francis Bosco. "He'll never let Axel sit on the jury," Katrin whispered to Jean.

But when Magnus asked if he had any objections, Francis shook his head. "No objection at all, Your Honor."

Jean turned to stare at Katrin and Isara; their eyes were as wide as her own. Axel had to let the bailiff's son, Bobby Christianson, usher him up to the jury box.

"It's okay," Katrin muttered. "There's still me and Isara. We can handle the awakenings."

Magnus reached into the silver bowl again. "The second randomly selected juror," he announced, "is . . . Isara Ratana!"

"Are you *kidding* me?" Katrin could barely keep her voice at a whisper.

"Don't worry," Isara said quietly. "I'll get out of it."

Magnus asked both lawyers if they had any objections to Isara serving on the jury. Neither did. But Isara had something to say.

"Excuse me, Mr. Mayor—I mean, Your Honor," he said, rising from his seat. "I'd like to request to be excused from jury duty. I have a lunch to cater, and I'll need to make final preparations during the trial."

Magnus cocked his blond head to one side. "Final preparations? But my guards tell me that the boxes you brought are filled with already-made sandwiches. Is that not the case?"

Clearly, one of the guards had sneaked a peek inside the boxes. Isara was stuck.

"I . . . er . . . yes, the sandwiches are the centerpiece of the lunch," he replied, "but there's also another element that I'll need to—"

"The sandwiches will be plenty for today. Take your seat in the jury box, Mr. Ratana."

As usual, Magnus was two steps ahead. Isara reluctantly sat beside Axel.

Magnus's hand went back into the bowl. Jean knew what name he would call out.

"Katrin Ash!"

"Sweet St. Polonius's Purple Parrot!" Katrin cursed, and the kids sitting nearby laughed again.

"Magnus King," she cried, jumping to her feet, "you cannot compel me to sit on this jury. I refuse. And I request that someone double-check the names listed on those papers he's been pulling from the bowl. It seems like *quite* the coincidence that every name pulled so far is . . . is . . ."

But there, her voice trailed off. What could she accuse Magnus of—purposely stacking the jury with Micah's friends? That didn't make sense.

The lawyers gave their approvals, and the bailiff came for Katrin. She put her hands on her hips.

"Officers Smuthers and Smuthers," Magnus said, "please escort Ms. Ash to the jury box."

In a moment, B&B were on either side of Katrin. When Bartleby reached for her elbow, Katrin shrank away as though he had tried to inject her with thistleberry poison.

"Don't you touch me," she snarled.

"Then march!"

Jean could tell that Katrin was finally out of ideas. It was another town charter rule: When you were selected for a jury, you *had* to judge the trial. If Katrin continued to object, Magnus could authorize B&B to drag her off to jail . . . or, worse.

"Go," Jean whispered. Clearly, Magnus was manipulating the jury selection—just not the way they'd expected. He must have learned quite a bit about their awakening scheme from his spy, and he'd sat on that information until the time was right.

Now, by sticking Micah's friends on the jury, Magnus was stopping them from waking the adults. It was such a clever solution that Jean would have admired it, if only it didn't spell total disaster for her plan.

Her own name would be called next.

But when it was, she'd become the fourth juror, meaning the majority of the seven-kid jury would be on Micah's side. They could vote to clear him of all charges. Then, once he was free, they'd regroup and figure out a new way to wake the sleepers.

So Jean smiled and gave Katrin a little nod to say *Don't worry. We've got this.* Katrin's eyebrows lifted, but she moved forward.

Magnus reached into the bowl, and Jean got ready to spring up the moment she heard her name. His eyes locked on hers as he drew the next slip.

"Caleb Marx!"

One of Axel's estranged cousins stood up. He'd be a vote against Micah. Jean realized now that Magnus would make her wait for her name; he wanted to see her squirm.

Sorry, Mr. Mayor, she thought, *but I know what you're up to. It won't work.*

The next name he called was Eliza Johanssen, whose resentment of Jean would surely extend to Micah. She was quickly approved by both attorneys, as was Alaria Daly, who had to leave her crossbow with one of her sisters.

Time to name the seventh juror.

Jean stared at Magnus, and he stared right back. His hand plunged into the bowl.

"Bartleby Smuthers!"

"WHAT?!"

The roar of outrage came from Jean's friends in the jury box, from Micah, and from Jean. She was on her feet without remembering having stood as Bartleby sauntered down the aisle to report for jury duty.

"Order in the court!" Magnus banged his gavel. "Bailiff, guards—see that the jury members, defendant, and observers behave."

Guards all around the room reached for their weapons. Some younger kids shrank back into their seats; one whimpered "Mama!"

Jean sat back down, dizzy. If Magnus was suspicious of her group, then why wouldn't he put them all on the jury? Why leave her, and only her, off of it?

Of course, this way the jury wasn't stacked for Micah. But still, if Magnus was afraid of her group taking action against him, why hadn't he made sure to neutralize every member?

Then, the answer came to her. Once Magnus had made Jean a waitress, he had all but ignored her; and when she'd offered herself up for arrest at the university, he'd let her go free. As part of a well-organized group, Jean worried Magnus. But on her own, she was just a girl who could barely spell. He didn't see her as a threat.

For a brief moment, Jean hoped that Cora might object to Bartleby sitting on the jury, but that didn't seem to be part of her (or Spike's) defense plan. So Bartleby climbed into the jury box, and Jean clenched her hands in her lap. Magnus was beaming; clearly he thought he'd succeeded in keeping the heat on Micah *and* stopping any challenge to his greater plan.

But you're wrong about that, Magnus, Jean thought. *And you're wrong about me, too.*

This fight wasn't over. Magnus had made a big mistake leaving Jean at large.

WITNESS LIST

For the prosecution:

- Bertha Smuthers,
  Interim Constable
- Bartleby Smuthers,
  Interim Deputy Constable
- Peter Rudberg,
  Interim Professor of Classics
  (and police informant)

For the defense:

- Jean Huddy,
  Interim Waitress

CHAPTER 28

Jean stood back up. No time to be nervous; the stakes were too high, and the new plan she was forming had no room for self-doubt.

"Hey!" she shouted. "This is *completely* unfair! There's no way Bartleby Smuthers is going to vote impartially in this trial. He's one of the people who arrested my brother!"

A murmur went through the crowd. A lot of kids were

actually nodding. Magnus's ears turned red, and he banged the podium with his gavel. "Order! Ms. Huddy, sit down!"

But the unexpected support fired Jean up.

"And speaking of fair," she yelled, "let's talk about these charges for a second. *Espionage?* Who exactly was my brother supposed to be spying for? Or against?"

Magnus banged even harder. "Jean Huddy, if you do not close your mouth and take your seat this instant—"

Would Mom close her mouth? Would Mom sit down?

Jean climbed up onto her chair.

"This town is sick and tired of your tyranny, Magnus King!" She was all but screaming. "You've misled voters, used the day care as your own personal poster factory, and swollen the police force to keep everyone in line. Well, we're over it!"

"Yeah!" several kids yelled. Jillian Seidel-Mitchell, Jack Perigee, and a few others Jean recognized from the Founders' Day play stood up.

"Free Micah Huddy!" cried one of Micah's classmates.

"Yay, Micah!" shouted another. Micah straightened a bit in his chair.

Magnus smashed his gavel so hard against the podium that it snapped in two; a kid in the front row ducked as the heavy head sailed through the air. At first Magnus didn't notice and kept hammering with the handle.

"Constable Smuthers!" he bellowed. "Jean Huddy is in contempt of court. Remove her!"

"Yes, sir!" Bertha made a beeline for Jean.

Jean did her best to look terrified—and with Bertha brandishing her weapon near Jean's good knee, it wasn't hard. "Okay, okay!" she yelled as she climbed down. "I'll go! Just don't hurt me!" Bertha poked her in the back with the end of her stick as Jean did an exaggerated limp out the door and into the hall.

Step one: She had gotten herself removed from the courtroom. Now for step two.

"I have to pee," she told Bertha.

"There's a toilet in the jail cell. And since your brother's about to get himself marooned, there's plenty of room for a new prisoner."

Jean had expected this. "There's no way I can make it all the way to the station. Ever since you busted my knee, I can hardly walk!"

Actually, her knee was feeling pretty good—but Bertha didn't know that. Jean stumbled and grabbed the wall.

"Axel Gorson's been driving me around," she continued, "but he's on the jury, he can't leave! And I drank a whole lot of tea before I came here this morning, so I *really* have to—"

"All right!" Bertha snapped. "Leaping lumpfish—anything to shut you up. We'll stop at the bathroom downstairs. Let's go."

She tapped Jean's back with the nightstick, and Jean lurched forward. "Katrin usually helps me walk," she said, "or sometimes Isara. But *they're* on the jury, so . . . I'll need someone else to lean on."

Bertha's eyes widened. "No way."

"Do you want me to go right here in the hallway?" Jean

whined. "Or maybe over there, in that corner by the mayor's office? I can probably make it *that* far on my own. . . ." She began to lumber across the hall, making a show of undoing her belt buckle.

"Wait—stop! Fine, you can lean on me."

Jean forced a smile. "Thanks." She slung an arm around her least favorite classmate.

As they tottered down the hallway together, Jean leaned heavily on Bertha. The girl strained to support her. When they got to the stairs, Jean made sure Bertha always stepped down before she did, so she could put all her weight onto Bertha each time.

While they descended, Jean did a careful inventory of the items hanging from Bertha's police belt—nightstick on her left hip, walkie-talkie on her right—and exactly how they were secured in place.

By the time they reached the lobby, Bertha was panting. The long tables sat empty now, and the town hall's main door was unguarded, since every other kid was in the courtroom.

They moved into the corridor that led to the bathrooms and the sleepers' room; Jean spotted the lunch boxes piled up outside of that door, right where they'd been left.

The ladies' room was a few feet away.

"I'm coming in to keep an eye on you," Bertha said, "so don't even try to keep me out."

"Keep you out?" Jean asked as Bertha opened the bathroom door. "I wouldn't dream of it!"

Then she put to work a technique she used to trick a sheep back into its stall. Standing tall on her own two feet, she let go of Bertha, who stumbled. Jean grabbed Bertha's waist as if to steady her, and with one quick yank of each hand liberated Bertha of her nightstick and walkie-talkie. Then Jean shoved her into the bathroom, pulled the door shut between them, and thrust the nightstick into the C-shaped door handle, locking it in place.

The door was thick, and Bertha's shouts came through as mere peeps. "Backup— My radio— Why, you little—!" She rattled at the door, but the nightstick stuck in place.

Jean dashed across the hall. Every second counted. She heaved the top box off the stack, balanced it in one arm using her best waitressing technique, and let herself into the sleepers' room.

A sour scent with mushroomy undertones greeted her: sleepers' sweat. She flipped on the light to reveal the rows of gently breathing adults and teenagers. Setting her box down on the first empty patch of carpet, she grabbed a squeeze bottle and got to work.

No question about who she would wake first. Jean scurried down the end row, eased herself onto her good knee, and gently parted Dr. Fields's lips. She didn't have time (or a scale) to weigh anyone, so she would have to estimate the doses. As soon as the first one was delivered, she cleaned off the nozzle with one of the sanitizing wipes Katrin had packed and moved on to the next person.

When the bottle ran out, Jean returned to the box for a new one. She'd made it all the way down one row of sleepers and halfway down a second when Bertha's walkie-talkie—which Jean had clipped to her own belt—buzzed. "Constable Smuthers? Constable Smuthers, come in, over."

Jean had expected this. If no one answered the check-in call, then a guard would be dispatched to investigate.

She pressed the button on the walkie-talkie, lowered her voice to imitate Bertha's, and hoped that the crackly reception would cover the rest. "Smuthers here. Over."

"Oh, good," said the voice at the other end. "This is Ben—I mean, Interim Officer Hansen. I'm supposed to check in on the status of the new prisoner. Do you need backup? Over."

Jean smiled, thinking of Bertha stuck in the bathroom. "Everything's under control, Hansen. She's locked up securely—no need for backup."

"Cool! I'll pass the word on to the big guy—I mean, Mr. Mayor. Okay, over and out."

Working as fast as she could, Jean finished the second row of sleepers. When she ran out of bottles, she got a new box. Bertha was still banging against the door of the bathroom.

It took Jean twenty minutes to make her way down the remaining rows, including two more trips for boxes. As she worked, she wondered what was going on upstairs. She should have asked Hansen for an update on the trial when he had radioed—though that might have raised suspicions.

The second-to-last person Jean dosed was Mr. Miller, all the while picturing his freezer of horrors. There was no one to wake up all the poor sharks and whales and high-altitude bears that he—or another poacher—had hunted illegally. It probably would have been a fitting punishment to leave the restaurant owner in his coma for a long time. But Jean contented herself with relieving Mr. Miller of the keys in his cloak pocket, so that someone else could get into his freezer after the awakening and see all the gory evidence.

Mr. Miller was laid out next to the mayor. Jean had saved him for the very end. She figured that if her calculations were off and she ran out of antidote, it wouldn't be such a tragedy for him to stay asleep a while longer. She still blamed Magnus for the actual hibernation, but she was sure that the mayor had known about Dr. Fields's findings—and hidden them. He'd failed in his duty to protect the citizens of St. Polonius from harm. That was almost as bad as if he had poisoned them himself.

There was enough left, though, to wake the mayor and her parents at home. Jean was just pulling the bottle from the mayor's mouth when she heard the sound of many of pairs of feet coming down the stairs.

How could the trial be letting out already? Jean checked her watch—less than an hour had passed since she'd escaped.

It must have been a bathroom break. And the bathrooms were right across the hall.

Pushing herself to her feet, Jean made for the light switch.

Someone was going to discover the jammed nightstick and free Bertha, and there was nothing she could do about that. All she could do was make sure that Bertha couldn't find Jean when she got out.

Jean flicked off the light as the footsteps reached the hallway outside. The room of sleepers plunged into darkness, and she groped the wall to keep her bearings. Crouching beside the door, she was just able to hear the conversation of a few approaching kids.

"I can't believe how short that was," one girl's voice said. "I thought the trial would go on for hours!"

Wait—the trial was over?

"Maybe it would've been longer if that kid's sister had been there to testify," said another girl. The words stabbed Jean in the gut. She doubted anything she said would have made much difference . . . but still, how must Micah have felt when Jean had gotten herself thrown out of the courtroom? Probably like his only ally—his only chance at a "not guilty" verdict—was gone. Jean could only hope that he would forgive her later.

"Hey, what's this?" a third voice cried. The kids had found the nightstick. "Who did this to the bathroom door?"

"Maybe it's out of order?"

"But there's no sign that says . . ."

Bertha's banging started up again. Jean heard a squeak as the bathroom door was pulled open.

"Where is she?" Bertha roared.

"Who?" asked one of the girls.

"Jean Huddy!"

"I don't know!" the girl squealed. "I haven't seen her since she left with you!"

"None of us have," said another voice.

"Then I need backup, *stat*!" Bertha cried. "Where are all the other guards?"

"Um," said the second voice, "back by the stairs . . ."

Bertha's boots pounded down the hallway, and Jean let out a long breath. Maybe Bertha would assume that Jean had run off; there was no way she'd look for her right across the hall. Still, Jean stayed crouched in the dark until she heard the group of girls leave the bathroom.

"Come on," said one of them. "You heard Mayor Magnus: The town charter says they only have to have a majority agree. What if that jury convicts the kid?"

No! Jean wanted to cry. She had counted on having more time to wake the adults before the trial ended. If Micah was convicted, Magnus would waste no time sentencing him—and he'd make sure the marooning happened right away.

Even if Judge Barrett declared a mistrial as soon as he woke up, what good would that do if Micah was already floating off into the North Sea?

The girls' footsteps faded down the hallway.

But wait—was that a whimper Jean heard? The rustle of a coat?

She rose and flicked on the light. There, two rows over, was Dr. Fields, sitting up straight, her hair wild and her eyes wide open.

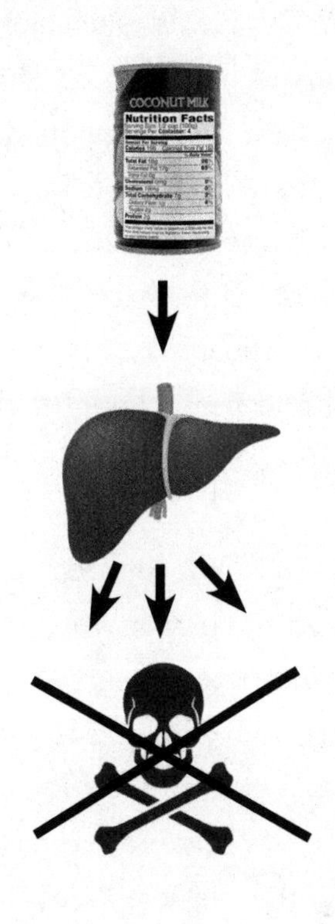

As Jean hurried across the room, a few more sleepers stirred. Dr. Fields was swaying slightly, and her skin had a greenish tinge. But she was trying to stand. Jean grabbed her outstretched hands to pull her upright.

"Jean Huddy," Dr. Fields whispered, her cracked lips breaking into a wide smile. "Great saints, am I glad to see you."

Jean could have wept with happiness. "Not half as glad as I am to see you!"

"Where am I?" Dr. Fields asked, looking around at all the other sleepers. "And what's going on?"

"You're at town hall," Jean explained. "And as for what's going on . . ." She did her best to fill her in very quickly on how the great hibernation had come about.

Dr. Fields took the information in calmly. "And how long have we all been asleep?"

"A week," Jean told her, "though I think it would have been much longer if we hadn't found your antidote formula for thistleberry poisoning."

Dr. Fields beamed. "You figured it all out," she murmured. "Even though the mayor worked so hard to suppress my discovery. I should have brought it to the public immediately, instead of trusting him to announce it on Founders' Day." She shook her head, and her long gray hair tumbled around her shoulders. "Where is that rat Theobald King?"

Jean nodded to the corner. "He's over there, next to Mr. Miller," she said. "I'm pretty sure Miller's the one who poached the high-altitude bear whose liver poisoned everybody—Isara Ratana and I discovered a horrible stash of other rare animal parts in the freezer at Ye Olde Mill Inn."

Dr. Fields nodded. "When the mayor and his son brought me samples to test, I asked him how on earth he'd gotten his hands on a liver so toxic. He said that a high-altitude bear must have wandered down to the sea-level hunting grounds and gotten killed by mistake. That sounded awfully convenient to me; I should have asked more questions."

Jean's toes were twitching in her boots. "Look," she said, "there's a lot more to this, but my brother, Micah, broke into your lab and stole the antidote formula. Magnus King caught him and put him on trial for espionage and treason, and the verdict's going to be read any minute, and if Micah's convicted—"

"Oh, no! And your parents?"

"Asleep at our farm."

"Then go to him!" Dr. Fields cried. "Leave this room to me. I'll make sure the others wake up safely and understand what's happened. I must—I had the information that could have prevented this catastrophe."

"Thank you!" Jean began to weave toward the door. Around her, eyelids fluttered and lips smacked. The grown-ups and teenagers of St. Polonius were all waking up, though it was a sight she couldn't linger to see.

Jean sped down the hall and started up the stairs. She'd nearly reached the top when she realized that she didn't know what to do when she reached the courtroom. The moment she showed her face, Magnus's guards would swarm. She might only have the chance to shout one sentence into the crowd.

It would have to be a good one.

Jean hustled toward the closed door, her knee starting to ache again. "Just one more step!" she told herself. "And one more after that!"

She grabbed the doorknob as Bartleby boomed, "We the jury, by a vote of four to three—"

Jean shoved the door open. It hit the wall with a bang, and every head in the room whirled around.

In the split second of silence, Jean saw: Micah and his

half-lawyer, the other attorney, and Bartleby Smuthers on their feet; Katrin with crossed arms and a murderous expression; Isara looking as though a teapot's worth of steam might erupt from his nostrils; and Axel's face streaked with tears.

"Guards!" Magnus cried.

"They're awake!" Jean shouted. "Downstairs, in the sleepers' room—our parents are all awake!"

Jillian and Jack shot up first, whooping and hollering along with several of Micah's classmates. They hurtled out of their seats, shoving to get out of the courtroom, and more kids followed.

"Order! Order!" Magnus smashed the podium first with his fist, then with his spelling-bee medal. But no one paid attention. Before any guards could reach her, Jean was surrounded by eager kids.

"Did you see my mom?"

"Is my dad up?"

"My sister's down there, did she ask for me?"

"Go see!" Jean cried. "But a lot of them are just waking up, so try to be patient, okay?"

The kids bolted away and thundered down the stairs. Two guards barreled toward Jean and she shrank back, but they ran right by her.

"Come back here!" Magnus shouted. "We have a verdict to deliver!"

But even the jurors were running away. As he shoved past her, Jean heard Bartleby calling into his walkie-talkie. "Bertha? Bertha, Mommy's awake!" Jean had abandoned the other walkie-talkie downstairs.

"Oh, you did it!" Katrin threw her arms around Jean. "I've gotta get down there, but I'll be back, okay?"

Axel took off, too, but Isara lingered for a moment. "Will you and Micah be all right . . . up here with *him*?"

Jean followed Isara's gaze to the judge's podium. Magnus still stood behind it, his eyes as wild as a rampaging bear's. "Don't worry," Jean said. "I can handle him."

Finally, she ran up to Micah.

"Jeannie," he croaked. His eyes were puffy, and his left hand was still tied to his chair. Jean undid the knot, then clutched him in a long embrace.

"Let's go find Rambo and get out of here," Micah said. But before they could take a step, a shadow fell across them.

Jean looked up into Magnus's seething face.

"That's my prisoner. You can't just take him away. He forfeited certain rights when he committed his crimes."

"And so did you," Jean said, "when you swapped the livers on Founders' Day and poisoned two hundred fifty people. Which to me sounds a lot more like *high treason* than searching for a cure." She took a deep breath. "You pretend you care about following every rule. But all along, you've bent the law whenever it suits you!"

"Oh, don't start with that poisoned-liver business again," Magnus scoffed. "Everyone knows that the only thing powerful enough to send the adults and teenagers into hibernation was a saintly miracle. And if they've woken up early . . . it must be because the saints wanted them to."

After all this, Magnus was still trying to blame the saints? Jean glared at him. "Our parents are awake because

I woke them, using Dr. Fields's antidote formula. And Isara and I saw you stashing the leftover liver in Mr. Miller's secret freezer, so don't pretend that there isn't any proof of what you did!"

In fact, Jean had no evidence that the cloaked figure at Ye Olde Mill Inn had been Magnus, but that was her best guess. She'd noticed the resemblance when she'd first seen him in judge's robes that morning. And she was pretty sure that when it came to hiding key evidence, Magnus wouldn't trust anyone but himself.

He went pale and grabbed the back of a chair. She was right!

"Look," Jean said, "just admit everything. Things will probably go better for you if you do."

"Go *better* for me?" Magnus sounded incredulous.

"Yes," Jean said. "If you confess what you did, and explain why, a jury will probably go easy on you. You're only a kid."

Magnus gripped the chair so tightly that it started to shake. "I am *not* only a kid. I am the *mayor* of St. Polonius-on-the-Fjord!"

"You *were*," Jean said, "but your interim mayorship is over."

Color flooded back into Magnus's face, and he pushed the chair away from him. "Who are you to be giving me advice?" he snapped. "You're just a waitress—and you're only *that* because you couldn't hack it as a sheep farmer! You probably can't even spell the word *interim. I-N-T-E-R*—"

"Oh, can the spelling!" Micah cried. "My sister's trying

to help you, though the saints know you don't deserve it. Why don't you listen?"

Jean gave Micah's shoulder a grateful squeeze. "Magnus," she said, "the sleepers are going to be angry that you put them in hibernation. But all those people—they were young once, too. Even awful old Mr. Miller. Which means that they'll understand what it feels like to be a kid, to want to impress your dad."

Magnus's voice grew quiet. "Is that why you think I did this? To *impress* my dad? Great saints, you're even stupider than I thought. My father is the worst mayor St. Polonius has ever seen!" Magnus pitched his voice to imitate Mayor King. " 'Oh, please, sir, won't you vote for my thistleberry proposal?' 'I'm begging you, madam—it will be so good for our town!' "

He shook his head. "Weak. Pathetic. First he let those National Thistleberry Council people push him around in the capital, convincing him that a big factory was what this town needed. And *then,* when they said they didn't have the money to build it, he invested our own! He couldn't say no." Magnus kicked another nearby chair, and it wobbled dangerously. "But the people of this town were going to have no problem saying no to my dad and voting down the proposal. That was why I had to do something. Not to *impress* him. To show him how a real mayor leads.

"A real mayor is strong. A real mayor maintains order! And when people dare to oppose him, a real mayor takes them down. I knew I could run this town better than he ever could—even if I had to take *him* down to do it."

Jean took a step back, pulling Micah with her.

"Did you think I planned to just hand the keys to town hall back to my dad the minute he woke up? No *way.* Adults would all be required to work at the thistleberry plant once it opened, right? Well, Dad would, too. Once everyone saw how much better I was at mayoring than he was, *I* would be made the permanent mayor of St. Polonius-on-the-Fjord. But you woke everyone up early!" Magnus's eyes flashed at Jean. "*You,* who weren't even supposed to be awake in the first place! You didn't eat your liver on Founders' Day—I knew that from the beginning. And that you were plotting against me this whole time." He stepped closer. "I tried to keep you busy by sticking you in that restaurant. I tried to keep you away from the information in Dr. Fields's lab. Today, I thought Bertha had finally taken care of you. But no. I guess a real mayor has to do *everything* himself!"

Magnus lunged at Jean, but she was ready. She leapt back, jerking Micah to her side. Magnus tripped over his robe, and his medal's ribbon caught on another chair. He crashed down and the chair tumbled on top of him, trapping him long enough for Jean and Micah to run.

They burst into the hallway as a posse of adults came charging up the stairs. "Where is he?" one cried. "The mayor's boy, who poisoned us all?"

Micah pointed to the courtroom. The group pushed through the door.

"What will happen to him?" Micah asked.

"Well," Jean said, "hopefully they'll start by taking away that stupid medal."

Micah grinned at her. She squeezed his hand, and they started down the stairs.

"Jeannie," Micah said, "did you really wake all the sleepers by yourself?"

Jean laughed. "Hardly! I had the formula from you, the antidote from Isara, and bottles from Katrin, all of which Axel transported in his truck. I just did a bunch of squeezing."

"Yeah, but you must've fought off Bertha Smuthers first."

Jean tapped her knee. "She had it coming."

The sounds of jubilation grew louder with each step, and Axel called to them from the bottom of the stairs. "Come on, guys! Dad's awake, and he says he'll drive us out to the farm to wake your parents!"

Jean and Micah sped up.

There were hundreds of adults and kids in the vast lobby, hugging and kissing and crying. Jean spotted a mop of teased hair moving through the crowd, and Katrin dashed up to them. "Mission accomplished!" she crowed.

"Your mom's awake?" Jean looked around. "Where is she?"

"Waiting by the door," Katrin said, "but that's not what I meant." She reached into her pocket and slid something out: shiny handle, sharp metal blades glinting through a plastic cap. It was the missing cordless razor from the salon.

"*You* took it?" Jean asked. "Sweet St. Polonius, Katrin—what have you done?"

Katrin leaned her head over the side of the bannister. "Behold, my masterpieces."

Two men were shuffling out of the sleepers' room, rubbing their eyes.

Theobald King and Burt Miller had new, short-buzzed hairdos with blocky letters carved into them, arcing all the way up over the tops of their heads.

"You know," Katrin whispered. "In case anyone wasn't sure who else was responsible for this whole thing."

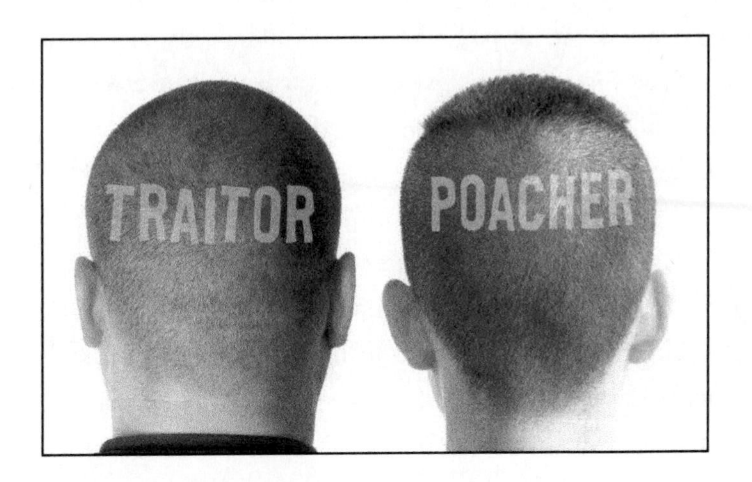

CHAPTER 30

People pointed at the mayor and Mr. Miller. Some laughed; others hissed. Jean wondered if, for the first time in their town's history, someone other than a King might be elected mayor—once the adults calmed down enough to vote.

"Come on," she said to Micah. "It's still Election Day. Mom and Dad will be mad if we don't wake them up in tim to do their civic duty!"

“Stop at my place first,” Katrin said, “so you can get Rambo.”

On the steps of town hall, Isara pulled away from his ecstatic parents and ran over to their group. “Jean, my parents want to thank you,” he said. “Your family, and Katrin’s and Axel’s, will get meals on the house anytime at the Tasty Thai Hut—though we understand if you’re coconutted out for a while.”

“Me?” Jean said with a smile. “Never!”

Isara grinned back and handed her a packet of Thai tea, tied up with a red ribbon. “For you.”

Their fingers brushed as Jean took it from him, and for once she was glad for the icy wind that always seemed to be buffeting their town. It cooled the blush rising up her neck.

Squeezing Jean, Micah, Katrin, Axel, Katrin’s mom, and Axel’s dad into the cab of the snowplow was tight, but today Jean didn’t mind being squashed close to her brother. Not after knowing he might have ended up alone in the North Sea, leagues away from her on a slab of ice.

The Ashes got out near the salon, and Katrin ran back with “St. Rambo.” Soon the plow was clearing the road to the Huddys’ farm. Axel looked like he might like to ram the accelerator with a stick a few times, but he didn’t complain.

Finally, the peaked roofs of the farm buildings came into iew. Steam rose from the chimneys, and Jean let out a sigh f relief—the geothermally powered feeding and watering stems were still working, and the house would still be hted.

Mr. Gorson turned in to the Huddys’ drive and parked

near the shed; as usual, Micah was out of the truck almost before it had stopped moving. Clutching her squeeze bottle of coconut milk, Jean raced into the house after him.

Their parents were right where they'd left them, side by side in their floor-bed. Dad was closer, so Jean knelt and slid the bottle's nozzle into his mouth first.

Then she gave Mom her antidote. While she delivered it, she thought about the election. Was there still time for someone new to run for mayor? Because the person who'd inspired her to stand up for St. Polonius-on-the-Fjord might make a good candidate.

Jean brushed a tendril of hair off Mom's forehead. "When you wake up," she whispered, "we're going to have to have a serious talk—about politics."

While they waited, Jean let Micah return Rambo to his pen and check on the other sheep. She also invited Mr. Gorson and Axel to come inside for a meal.

It felt strange to be puttering around a kitchen alone after so many days of working beside Isara. As exhausting as it had been, she was going to miss her job at the Tasty Thai Hut. Maybe, if Mom ended up spending more time at town hall, they could all eat dinner with the Ratanas at the restaurant once in a while.

She thawed lamb stew from the freezer and put water in the kettle. When the water boiled and Axel's dad asked if Jean had any thistleberry tea, she told him about Dr. Fields's latest findings. If he was going to be driving them all back to town, it was better to be safe than sorry. "How about a cup of Thai tea instead?" she asked. Mr. Gorson said that would be fine.

It was while she was taking a second pot of water off the burner for refills that Jean heard Micah shout from the living room.

"You're awake! Dad, Mom—you won't believe what happened! Magnus King drugged all the adults and teenagers in town using bear liver, but Jeannie figured everything out and saved us all!"

Smiling, Jean set the kettle back on the stove. There was more to it than that, but still, she had finally done something her family—and her town—could be proud of.

And she ran to welcome her parents back to the waking world.

TO:
JEAN HUDDY
WHO SAVED OUR TOWN,
ST. POLONIUS

ACKNOWLEDGMENTS

Loud roars of appreciation for the following people:

Ammi-Joan Paquette, who couldn't have found a better home for this book. I thank you to the end of the Infinity Ice Rink and back. Wendy Lamb and Dana Carey, I can't imagine a more astute, encouraging, and *fun* editorial team. I will keep trying to write to your high standards. Crispy fried bananas for everyone!

Many thanks to the rest of the Penguin Random House team who have made this book a work of art: jacket designer Katrina Daemkoehler, interior designer Trish Parcell, chapter opener designer Sarah Hokanson, and illustrator Rebecca Green.

My fellow writers who critiqued drafts of the manuscript and encouraged me to keep going with it—Ann Bedicheck, Rebecca Behrens, Jennifer Chambliss Bertman, Jenny Goebel, Joy McCullough-Carranza, Jeannie Mobley, and Lauren Sabel—thank you. Melanie Crowder, Jessica

Lawson, and Joshua McCune, thanks for the key feedback on the excerpts you read.

Narisa Ratana-Chen, Sukdith Punjasthikul, and Mehta Punjasthikul were extremely generous with their time, sharing their knowledge of Thai food, culture, and immigration issues with me. Any errors in these areas are mine alone.

Tommy Bottoms answered my questions about sheep behavior and rearing in incredible detail (though I admit that I still chose to depart from reality in a couple of places for narrative effect). Thank you, Tommy, and the farmer and veterinarian you consulted on my behalf.

The sigil that hangs over my desk says *A Dairman Always Meets a Deadline*. Thanks to Brooke for that. And thanks to my little one for giving me a whole two days off after turning in my draft before making your debut in this world. (Deadline met!) Special thanks to Alicia Roman, whose babysitting helped me meet my revision deadline, too.

Andy, without your mad road-tripping skills, I never would have visited the town in Iceland that inspired the setting for St. Polonius-on-the-Fjord. Looking forward to many more years of edge-of-my-rental-car-seat adventures with you.

ABOUT THE AUTHOR

If all the adults had fallen asleep when Tara Dairman was twelve, she would have gone straight to the library to read about far-flung places. Now that she's an adult herself, Tara travels far and wide and has visited more than ninety countries. She has a BA in creative writing from Dartmouth College and is the author of the All Four Stars series of foodie adventures for young readers. Visit her online at taradairman.com or follow @TaraDairman on Twitter.